WOLF AT THE DOOR

BOOKS BY BARBARA CORCORAN

A Dance to Still Music
The Long Journey
Meet Me at Tamerlaine's Tomb
A Row of Tigers
Sasha, My Friend
A Trick of Light
The Winds of Time
All the Summer Voices
The Clown
Don't Slam the Door When You Go
Sam
This Is a Recording
Axe-Time, Sword-Time
Cabin in the Sky
The Faraway Island
Make No Sound
Hey, That's My Soul You're Stomping On
"Me and You and a Dog Named Blue"
Rising Damp
You're Allegro Dead
A Watery Grave
August, Die She Must
The Woman in Your Life
Mystery on Ice
Face the Music
I Am the Universe
A Horse Named Sky
You Put Up with Me, I'll Put Up with You
The Hideaway
The Sky Is Falling
The Private War of Lillian Adams
The Potato Kid
Annie's Monster
Stay Tuned
Family Secrets
Wolf at the Door

WOLF
at the
DOOR

Barbara
Corcoran

A JEAN KARL BOOK

ATHENEUM 1993
New York

MAXWELL MACMILLAN CANADA
Toronto

MAXWELL MACMILLAN INTERNATIONAL
New York Oxford Singapore Sydney

ATHENEUM
Macmillan Publishing Company
866 Third Avenue
New York, NY 10022

MAXWELL MACMILLAN CANADA, INC.
1200 Eglinton Avenue East
Suite 200
Don Mills, Ontario M3C 3N1

Macmillan Publishing Company is part of the Maxwell
Communication Group of Companies.

First edition
Printed in the United States of America
10 9 8 7 6 5 4 3 2 1
The text of this book is set in Weiss.

Library of Congress Cataloging-in-Publication Data
Corcoran, Barbara.
Wolf at the door / Barbara Corcoran. — 1st ed.
p.   cm.
"A Jean Karl book."
Includes bibliographical references.
Summary: Living in the shadow of her beautiful and talented
younger sister, Lee cares for a wolf pack that needs protection
from cattle ranchers.
ISBN 0-689-31870-7
[1. Sisters—Fiction. 2. Wolves—Fiction.
3. Montana—Fiction.]
I. Title.
PZ7.C814Wk   1993
[Fic]—dc20   92-45108

For Katie Tinkham

If all the beasts were gone, men would die from a great loneliness of spirit. For whatever happens to the beasts also happens to man. All things are connected.

—*From a letter written by Chief Seattle of the Suwamish tribe to President Franklin Pierce in 1855*

ACKNOWLEDGEMENTS

I owe this book and the fun of writing it to Dorothy Patent, who once took me to a place in northwestern Montana where a large pack of wolves was being protected and cared for. It was an unforgettable experience.

My thanks to Andrea Dixon, who has kept me supplied with books and pictures of wolves from her home in Alaska.

All of us who care about wolves owe a debt to Defenders of Wildlife. I am especially grateful to their local representative, Hank Fischer, who has provided me with information and help.

And special thanks to Linda Walch, without whose secretarial skill this book would have been still limping along.

The characters, including the wolves, are entirely fictitious. The town of Bigfork is real, but I have taken a few liberties with it for the sake of the story.

CHAPTER 1

I bet you can't go right across the field without stepping on a dandelion," my sister, Savannah, said.

"I bet I don't want to."

"It's a matter of grace and control," she said. "I'll bet I could walk from here to Flathead Lake without stepping on one."

"Why don't you?" I said.

My sister is eleven, going on twelve, two years younger than I am. Sometimes she sounds like she's about six, and other times she could be sixteen. My mother says I'm thirteen going on thirty-nine, but she's forgotten all the problems you have to deal with at my age. Like a kid sister who is beautiful and talented and, when the time is right, oozing with charm. I am none of those things.

Until I was seven we lived right here in Missoula,

Montana, on the other side of town. My father was a deejay at a radio station. When the station folded, he wanted to go back to the university radio-TV school, but he couldn't afford it. Some old buddy told him he could get good training in the army, so one day he went and joined up, without a yes, no, or whatever to my mom or anybody. So my sister and I became army brats.

During basic training we lived in a little house off base in Georgia, and it wasn't bad. Then he was sent to a base a hundred miles from Fairbanks, Alaska, where he worked at the army radio station. We had to live on the base, and my sister kept getting chest colds; it was dark as night all winter, and it got to fifty and sixty below a lot of the time. So after one year of that, Mom took us kids to Laguna Beach, California, to live with our grandmother till Dad was reassigned.

Finally he got assigned to Germany, and we all went. We had to stay pretty much on the base, which was near Frankfurt. We went to school on the base, and it was really just like an American colony. Even so, we were homesick most of the time.

And now it had all come to a happy end. My dad was out of the army, and we'd moved back to Montana.

My sister turned and yelled at me, "What are you standing there for like the Statue of Liberty?"

I started after her, stepping on dandelions because they're everywhere. I'm supposed to feel guilty? Next week they'll be fluffballs, and then weeds.

"Remember how it was at Nonny's when Dad was in Alaska?"

"Of course I remember. Swimming pool, beach, orange trees. So?"

She couldn't remember it the way I did, though. I was Nonny's first grandchild, and I named her that. She liked it. She said it reminded her of "Hey, nonny, nonny-o," and made her feel cheerful. Nonny is quite a famous actress, although she's getting old now.

"Remember Alaska?" On a spring day like this, with the creek running full and school just out, why was I thinking of Alaska?

"I don't want to remember Alaska." Savannah shivered and coughed. Just lately she'd worked up a very good fake cough, because in her school play she played some kid who was supposed to be dying. If Mom scolds her about her room being in a mess, she does her cough act.

I jumped a puddle from last night's rain, feeling good. The lilacs were out; chokecherry bushes bloomed all over like clumps of snow. And there was real snow on the highest peaks north of us.

In the back of my mind there was a small worry, though. My father had a job he loved, getting a new local TV station going with another guy. He got to do everything, from filming to broadcasting the local news. But the cable company in the area was fighting the station, and they might have to shut down.

I picked a jonquil from a little bed of flowers and made a wish: Don't make us move again. Let us stay right here in our brown, rented house one block from the river.

A couple of kids went by and yelled, "Hey, Van!"

Most people call my sister Van or Vannie. I call her

Savannah. I don't know why Mom couldn't have given me Nonny's name. I came first. I'm plain Lee, not even Leontyne or Leonora.

Ahead of me, Savannah made a flying leap in her new green-and-white running shoes and landed with a sickening squinch in a puddle of muddy water up to her ankles.

"Hey!" I yelled at her. "You knocked over five dandelions."

Her feet made sounds like a dying fish as she stepped free.

"It's your fault," she said. "I'm going to tell Mom you pushed me."

She would, too, and Mom might possibly believe her. It's just a great big wonderful world we live in.

CHAPTER 2

I smelled trouble the minute my father walked into the kitchen. For one thing, he was early. He and Joe worked practically day and night at the station, and if he had an hour free he went out to the fitness center and swam and lifted weights. He was almost never home for dinner.

But here he was, strolling in while my mother was chopping celery for one of her good salads. She looked up, at first surprised, then alarmed.

"Daddy!" Savannah threw herself at him with her usual gusto, as if she hadn't seen him for years. With me or even sometimes with Mom she can be cranky and stubborn, but you let our father appear on the scene and this child is an angel straight from the firmament. I just wish he'd smile at me the way he does at her.

But this time he didn't smile. He flopped into a chair.

"Merry Christmas," he said on that third day of June. "I have just joined the great army of the unemployed."

My mom sagged against the sink and said, "Oh, no."

"Yep. They plowed us under. Never fight the system; you lose."

"You don't mean that," Mom said.

"Well, we lost this time."

"Never mind, Daddy," Savannah said. "You can join the army again, and we can go somewhere nice."

"Over my dead body," I said.

"And mine," Mom said.

"The army is cutting down, honey." He gave Savannah a weak smile. "Not taking on. Well, how do the want ads in the *Missoulian* look?"

Except for Savannah nobody talked much during dinner.

Finally my mother said, "Well, thank heaven for the railroad." When Savannah was three, Mom put her in nursery school and answered an ad for a railroad dispatcher. Her field is biology, but she met Dad when she was halfway through her doctorate, and got married instead of finishing. Anyway, they loved her at the railroad, and when we came back last fall, they rehired her right off.

"There's always unemployment," Dad said.

"The ads in the *Missoulian* are big on busboys for McDonald's and Burger King," Mom said, "or addressing envelopes at home." She was trying to make a joke, but she was upset. She'd hated all the moving around we did.

"You can be a house husband," I said.

He gave me a dirty look. "Actually McDonald's might do to tide me over. I'm a pretty good cook, you know."

"Terrific!" Savannah cooed. "We can get free hamburgers."

"Savannah," I said, "shut up." And for once nobody told me not to pick on my little sister.

We were sent to our rooms early, which meant there was a family conference coming up.

Savannah perched on my bed. I wanted to throw her out, but I thought maybe she was more scared than she let on.

"We can sell this house for big bucks," she said. "Real estate is up. And we can go live on Dad's land near the lake."

"One, we don't own this house. Two, real estate is down. Three, the only thing on Dad's land is a tent."

"I love tents," she said.

"Mosquitoes? Blackflies? Snakes? Bears? Wintertime?"

Dad had acquired quite a big chunk of land when we were little: thick woods, a few miles from the north end of Flathead Lake. He packed his tent in there and went fishing when he had time. We'd stayed there sometimes for a week at a time. It was fun, but you don't move a family of four into a tent in the woods.

A lot of grown-up talking went on for the next few days. They usually stopped when we showed up. Children are always the last to know. But finally they called us into the living room.

Dad was looking pleased for the first time in days.

"Well," he said, "I've got a job, kids. Furthermore, I've got a plan you're going to love."

I had this feeling I wasn't going to love it.

"I've got myself a job, a good one. Newscaster at one of the bigger TV stations. In Kalispell."

"Daddy, terrific!" A bear hug from Savannah.

"What's the plan?" I couldn't see him commuting to Kalispell.

He looked at his watch. "Any minute I expect a call from your grandmother. My partner and friend in need." He was smiling.

"I don't know why you had to drag Mother into it," Mom said.

"I needed moral support. Plus a small loan. Kids, we're moving to the great Montana wilderness. To our land in the woods."

"I'm not moving anywhere," I said, but the ringing phone drowned me out.

Dad grabbed it. "Hello, darling!" When he talks to Nonny, he talks like some Hollywood character. "Wonderful to hear from you. Perfect timing. My wife is looking mournful, and my older child is making sounds of rebellion." He listened a minute and beamed. "Marvelous! Leave it to you! Listen, will you tell your daughter? Great. I love you." He handed the phone to Mom.

I couldn't tell from her face what was going on, and she was mostly saying, "Oh, I see," and, "Well, I can't say it thrills me. I like my job here, you know." Then she closed her eyes and held the phone a little away from her ear for a minute. "All right, Mother. I guess we've covered this before. Yes, I'll put her on."

Savannah leaped for the phone, but Mom said, "Lee first."

"Lee, darling," Nonny was saying, "you are going to love this new development, and it's so good for your dad

8

to get into just the work he trained for. I know you're happy about it."

"I don't want to leave Missoula, Nonny," I said.

"Darling, you'll only be an hour or so away."

"Two hours. There's only a tent up there in the woods."

"Wait till you hear!" Nonny is always so enthusiastic. "I got Sarah onto the problem." Sarah is her longtime secretary. "She's found this marvelous man in the Bitterroot Valley who does prefab woodsy-type houses, moves the parts to the site and just puts them together. Incredible, isn't it?"

"Incredible," I said.

"I knew you'd love it once you got used to the idea. Now let me speak to darling Savannah. I love you, Lee."

I gave the phone to Savannah and looked at my mother.

"We have to fight this," I said.

"How?" Mom looked as if she might burst into tears, something she almost never does.

"You can't do this to us, Dad," I said, but he wasn't listening. He was watching Savannah, eager and happy. Three of a kind: Nonny, Savannah, and Dad.

"Your grandmother is paying for it," Mom said. "It's already ordered."

"Well, I'm not going." I slammed out of the house.

CHAPTER 3

The day before the Fourth of July. Two cheers. The last pickup load roared off, Dad driving, Savannah as copilot. The two of them had been up at our New Home almost every day, "getting things ready." Savannah wanted to tell me all about it, but I wouldn't listen.

I'd just sat on the porch watching the house get emptier and emptier, the secondhand-store man and the storage man coming, and bags and bags taken to the trash cans. All I could think was, there goes my life again.

Now I was sitting beside the creek. It was running fast and noisily, the way I love it, and leaving it was going to break my heart.

I knew Mom was looking for me. It was time to go. Her blue Toyota was packed to the roof. She'd been worrying how she'd find a job. How do you find a job in the forest? Open a retirement home for senior chipmunks?

I took in a deep breath, like it was my last, all those good smells of river and flowers and trees. Fluff was beginning to drift off the cottonwoods like soft, dry snow.

I groaned out loud. And there was my mom right behind me.

"I'm sorry." She sat down beside me. "I know how you feel."

"Then why didn't you just say no?"

"I said *no* till I was hoarse. I put my foot down. I put both feet down. Equal rights, ha! It's never equal. Something has to give. Sure, I could refuse. Then what? Split up the family? My own mother ganged up on me. She never did like telling people I was a dispatcher, her only daughter with half a Ph.D. I never could convince her I wasn't standing out by the tracks waving red and green lanterns."

We both laughed.

"She thinks living in the forest is a wonderful idyll." Mom stood up. "Well, before we go, let's drive over to Goldsmith's and order the very biggest sundae they've got, with twelve kinds of sauce, whipped cream, and two cherries."

"Hey! Can we?"

"Why not? I hope I have that much control over my life."

"Savannah will turn green when she hears this."

Usually Mom would say I shouldn't gloat over my sister, but this time she laughed. "We'll show 'em."

So we spent an hour on the wide porch overlooking

the Clark Fork River, pigging out on Goldsmith's ice cream. And Mom had a cup of cappuccino.

"Actually, you know," she said, "Kalispell isn't all that far from where we'll be. And Bigfork is really close. And there's Flathead Lake. I mean you can't get any bigger than Flathead Lake."

We both giggled. Dad was born on the west side of the lake, and he always talked about it like it was his private lake. It is the biggest lake west of the Great Lakes. I grew up hearing that.

Being with Mom one-on-one like this almost made me stop feeling sad. If only Savannah would keep going right up into the Klondike, and I could have my mother to myself. Maybe even my father would pay some attention to me.

"I guess bears probably come right up to the cabin," I said.

"Think small." We went out and got into the car. "Think squirrels and small owls and butterflies."

As we were pulling out, a friend of Mom's ran up to the car. It was my friend Holly's mom. "Are you really going, Anita?"

"Real as real can be."

"Listen, we're going to miss you at the book club. And Lee, Holly cried half the night."

"Tell her I'll write." Holly was the one close friend I'd had time to make.

"You're going to have a wonderful adventure."

"You bet," Mom said. "I'll send you a snapshot of Bigfoot."

I hung out the window all the way up Front Street, past the library where the nice librarians saved books for me, over onto Broadway past the courthouse, past the motels. Then I rolled up the window and shut my eyes for a long time.

After a while my mother said, "Let's think of the place we would most like to be going to in the whole world, someplace we've never been."

I thought about it. "The English Channel Islands." I had done a report on them at school, and they sounded nice.

"Okay. Tell me everything you know."

We were in Ronan before I finished talking. We stopped for Indian fry bread.

The mountains in front of us looked so close, jagged and capped with snow.

"Is there a stove in this shack?" I asked.

Mom looked at me. "Honey, you really should have gone and looked at it. It's a big cabin. It's got everything. Three bedrooms, two baths, fridge, stove, freezer—"

"You're kidding! Is that for real?"

"Your grandmother paid for it, and you know it's nothing but the best for her. We tried to tell you about it, but you wouldn't listen. It's so big, the men who delivered the logs had to break down small trees along that trail. It's got a lot of built-ins: bookshelves, bureau drawers, all that. The rooms are small, but you'll have your own."

"Is that old fence still there, the one Dad thought would keep hunters out?"

"He's been repairing it. He thought he might raise goats."

"Goats! They stink."

"Well, they aren't there yet."

From the look on my mom's face, I figured maybe they

never would be. Goats are kind of cute, but they get into everything.

"It *is* a lot smaller place than we're used to, though, and Lee, I hope you'll try to get along better with your sister. You're the older, and you should take some responsibility."

I couldn't think of an answer to that, so I kept still.

About half an hour later we stopped at Allentown for a Coke, and I figured this was probably the last detour we could take to put off getting there; but a little later, on a dirt road that led toward the mountains, I saw a scrawled sign, tacked to a tree, that said ZOO, 2 MI.

"Mom, a zoo! Can we go look?"

She frowned. "I thought they passed a law against those tacky little roadside places. They never took decent care of the animals."

"Maybe we should check it out. If the animals aren't treated right, you could report it." My mother likes animals a lot, all kinds.

She backed up and turned down this bumpy old road. The place we came to was tacky, even for a roadside tourist trap. There was a small house looking ready to fall down, and an old barn that really was falling down. Next to the road were these cages. One of them had a couple of rabbits, another one had a small red fox, and behind them in a little wider cage was a wolf! They all looked in bad shape, but the wolf was the worst, really skin and bones.

My mom made an angry noise in her throat and got out of the car fast. A trampy-looking guy and a big old mangy dog came out of the house. "One dollar to see the animals." He had a high, squeaky voice, and he needed a shave.

"I can see them from here," my mother said. "They're half starved." My mother is only five foot three, 108 pounds, but she can sound really tough.

"Now looka here." The man's two-tooth smile faded. "I don't like trouble. A man has to earn a living best way he can."

"Well, there are better ways than this. Look at that wolf. She doesn't even have any water." Mom opened the cage and took out a dirty old water dish and marched over to a hose that lay beside the house. The wolf just shrank back in her cage. She looked young, but she had the saddest eyes I ever saw.

"Here! What you think you're doin'?"

My mother didn't bother to answer. She filled the dish and gave it to the wolf, and then she dragged the hose over and filled the dishes in the other cages.

"These animals need food," she said.

"I ain't got hardly enough money to feed myself."

My mother pulled a ten-dollar bill from her wallet and shoved it at him. "You buy some meat for those animals. And take care of them. I'm going to check back in a week to make sure you do. There are laws about these things, you know."

He grabbed the ten, and I could almost see him counting the bottles of booze it would buy. My mother was throwing her money away.

"One week," my mother said. "I'll be back." She started toward the car.

"You some kind of a pre-reservation freak, come in here bossin' me around?" He looked real mean.

"You better believe it."

The man said something to his dog, and it started slouching toward us, growling. My mother is not afraid of dogs, even mean ones, but I got in the car real quick.

Mom stopped, looked at the dog, and said, "Oh, don't be ridiculous."

That dog stopped in his tracks and whined. I wasn't surprised; I've seen my mother with dogs like that before. But the man's eyes really bugged out.

Mom slammed the car door, made a neat gravel-spitting U-turn, and drove fast down the road, raising a cloud of dust.

"One week," she said. "I give that bum one week."

Sometimes I'm really impressed with my mother.

CHAPTER 4

Just before we got to Bigfork we turned onto a narrow
dirt road. I had to admit it had been a pretty drive along
the lakeshore. The sky and the lake were the same shade
of blue. There were some sailboats far out on the lake. Tall
pines grew right down to the shore. I'd heard there were
some really nice summer homes in there, but you couldn't
see them.

I was bracing myself for our new home. At least we
were still in Montana. I could be glad about that.

The trail had big roots sticking up, and potholes you
could fall into. I couldn't imagine how they'd gotten all that
lumber here if the house was as big as Mom said.

We were heading east, away from the lake, into thick
woods where the trees were so tall, they shut out a lot of

the sunlight. "This isn't going to be like Alaska, is it?" I said. "Dark all the time?"

"Your father has cleared a big area in front of the house."

It was funny to hear it called a house. In my mind it was a tacky little shack.

"Looks like they had trouble getting the trucks in." Mom pointed to some torn-up bushes and small trees.

We came to a fork and turned right.

"Where does that other trail go?"

"Somebody on the other side of the woods has a sheep ranch, your father said."

I was trying not to feel nervous.

"It was neat the way you told that old guy off."

"Your father would say it was foolish. Those tough old boys can get mean."

"Savannah would have fainted at that dog. I was scared myself."

Savannah had been attacked by a Doberman when she was little, and she'd never gotten over being scared of dogs.

We hit a pothole and the wheels spun, but Mom backed and forwarded till we got going again.

All of a sudden we came to a big clearing. She pointed.

"There's your new home, sweetheart."

"That's *it*?"

"That's it."

"Wow!" It was really about the neatest house I'd ever seen, long and low, built of logs that had been stained dark so they blended right into the forest that came down close in back. In front there was a cleared space.

She beeped her horn, and we got out. No sign of anyone. Then Savannah popped out of the trees, red bandanna tied around her face, all but her eyes, and waving a pistol at us.

"Your money or your life," she shrieked. "Happy Fourth of July!" She squirted the gun, and I got a faceful of cold water.

I yelled, and Savannah screamed with delight.

Mom said, "Savannah McDougall, don't you ever, ever point a gun at anyone again. You hear me?"

"Oh, Mom, it's only water."

"I don't care if it's champagne. You are never to do that again."

I was mopping my face, and I really felt like slugging her.

"Speaking of champagne!"—my father sauntered out of the cabin looking like he was welcoming us to the Land of Oz—"I happen to have a pitcher of homemade lemonade, made in the shade."

"I squeezed the lemons," Savannah said.

I took a load of stuff from the car into the cabin. Might as well see the inside.

Things were sitting wherever Dad and Savannah had dropped them, but in spite of the confusion, it was nice. The only trouble was, we were going to be living practically on top of one another.

"Well, it's going to be a touch crowded," Mom said.

"Like L. A. at rush hour," I said.

My father glared at me. "Lee, you are the biggest grouch I've ever met."

I wanted to say, "I really love it," but he wouldn't have believed me. The trouble is, I really love *him*, no matter how much he bugs me or I bug him. I'd give my right arm if he'd smile at me the way he was smiling at Savannah just then.

CHAPTER 5

Before we even had time to catch our breath, Dad took us into Kalispell to show us his TV station, and then out for pizza and down to the lake to watch the fireworks. Fireworks beside water are extra beautiful. It was a real *ahh!* night.

Savannah had already staked out the bedroom she wanted, so when I woke up next morning, it was in the little room facing the forest behind us.

At first I couldn't figure out what the sound was. Then I saw my mother sawing away on a two-by-four. Dad had fixed up the fence all the way around the woods behind the cabin, but he always leaves something unfinished. This time it was the gate. Mom was out there in her oldest jeans and a sleeveless T-shirt, making a gate.

I looked around my room, which was full of unpacked

suitcases and books and clothes and general junk. My framed studio photo of Nonny taken right after World War II leaned against the wall. I had a million pictures of her, but that was my favorite. There wasn't going to be room for many pictures in this room though—too many built-in drawers. There was even a nineteen-inch built-in TV with a CD player right below and a shelf for tapes. It was really neat the way whoever built this thing had economized on space.

I got up and measured for Nonny's photo. It fit, just barely. I stood looking at it, wondering what she would think of this "home" she had paid for. She'd probably love it; she likes ingenuity.

She lives in Laguna Beach now, and it was wonderful staying with her while Dad was in Alaska. The beach was great. And we had a private tutor, whom we liked a lot. Our schooling, as Nonny says, is enough to give you the vapors.

I took a shower in the tiny bathroom and put on a clean pair of jeans and a T-shirt with a grizzly bear's head and UNIVERSITY OF MONTANA on it. I thought about that poor little wolf we'd seen the day before. She hadn't looked as if she'd last a week. People ought to be shot for treating animals that way.

After breakfast I helped Mom with the gate, and then the three of us—Mom, Savannah, and I—walked the property line, checking out the fence. It was a much bigger piece of property than I had remembered.

From the eastern limit we could see where the woods ended in pastureland. Mom said she thought that was where the sheep rancher lived.

Mom told us the names of trees and ferns and fungi,

and identified birdcalls. I forget them as fast as I learn them, and Savannah doesn't even listen, but Mom was having a good time. Nonny was right—Mom really ought to be using all she knew about biology and botany.

Dad came home that night enthusiastic about his job, and the rest of the week went by fast, getting settled and taking walks and building birdhouses that Mom wanted to put in the trees near our house.

Dad had signed up both Savannah and me with a swimming class in Bigfork. Savannah began going nearly every day. The first time she conned Mom into taking her, but then Mom made her ride her bike. It wasn't all that far, although to hear Savannah you'd think it was a hundred miles. I went a few times, and it was a nice pool, but I needed time to psych out situations and people.

One week after we'd been to that zoo place, Mom asked Dad to swap cars with her. He never asks questions or argues about things like that, so off he went in Mom's car.

Mom said to Savannah, "I'll drive you to the pool today, and pick you up. I may be a little late, but you stay right there." To me she said, "I'll need your help."

And I knew we were going to the zoo man's.

After we left Savannah we went to a pet store, and Mom bought the biggest dog carrier they had. I didn't know what she had in mind, but my guess was that she was thinking of taking the wolf and the fox to the Humane Society. She had that concentrated look that means "Don't bother me now with questions."

She drove around to the back of the supermarket and made a deal with the butcher for a lot of slightly old meat and bones. Then we walked along the street till she saw a window with a NOTARY PUBLIC sign. It was some kind of secretarial place. We went in.

"I need a couple of papers notarized," Mom said.

"Okay. Have a seat." The woman smiled at me.

Mom took out two sheets of paper from her purse. "I guess a notary has to read what she notarizes, and this may sound odd to you. I can explain it if you like."

The woman laughed. "As long as it's legal, it's none of my business."

"Well, it may bend the law just a tad," Mom said. "But it's in a good cause."

The two sheets were identical. While the notary read one, I leaned over and read the other. I was as surprised as she probably was. Here's what it said:

I, Anita McDougall, resident of Bigfork, Montana, do on this day of July 11, 1993, purchase from A. Dolan, owner of the so-called zoo on East Ponderosa Road, south of Bigfork, for the sum of fifty dollars, made out by check payable at the Montana Bank of Missoula, one young female wolf in severely neglected condition, and one red fox in similar condition. I also reserve the right to release from confinement two white rabbits.

Anita McDougall
RFD Box 1, Bigfork, Montana 59911

The woman said, "I've never been more glad to notarize anything. I've seen that place." She had Mom sign both copies, and then she stamped the seal on them. "You probably could have done it for twenty dollars."

"Maybe, but I want a minimum of trouble."

"What are you going to do with them?"

"Take them home till I can get them into better shape. Then I don't know."

"The fox would make out all right on his own. I don't know about a lone wolf. Some people around here are pretty antiwolf. They think they might prey on their livestock." She shook her head as Mom started to pay. "My pleasure. And good luck to you."

Mom thanked her.

Up till now I hadn't been sure what we were going to do, but now that I knew, I could hardly wait. *That* was why we had been so careful with that new gate to the fenced-in woods. We were going to bring home a wolf and a fox!

CHAPTER 6

I began to get nervous as we turned down the road toward the zoo. I glanced up to see if Dad's rifle was in the gun rack.

"It's not loaded." Mom had seen me look up. "The shells are in the glove compartment. As you know, I don't like guns. Anyway, I don't intend to go in there and murder Mr. Dolan, you know."

"But if he gets tough, you could pull out the gun. He won't know it isn't loaded."

She gave me a withering look. "So Mr. Dolan and I face each other with guns, like *High Noon*, and we fire, only mine is unloaded, so I'm the one who falls over dead. Take a word of advice: Never make a threat you can't carry out."

"How did you know his name is Dolan?"

"It's on his mailbox, Dr. Watson."

I laughed. "Okay, Sherlock."

The pickup groaned as we hit a pothole. A sack of meat fell over with a clunk.

"Do you think we'll get away with this?"

"I have a feeling Mr. Dolan will do a lot for fifty bucks. And you don't exactly see a stream of tourists beating a path to his zoo."

We were close to the place now, and my hands felt sweaty.

"I want you to stay in the car," she said, "unless I ask you for help."

I thought of that mean dog. "Okay."

She stopped by the yard. The place looked worse than ever. The rabbits were there, but the fox cage was empty. I could see the wolf lying down, and I prayed she wasn't dead.

Mom got out and marched up the rickety steps to the front door of the house. She knocked on the door. Nothing happened. I opened the pickup door so I could get out quickly if she needed help. She knocked again, loudly, and called, "Mr. Dolan?" Nothing.

There was no sign of a car, although there could have been one behind that old barn. After one more bang on the door, she went back and checked on the wolf.

Then she came over to the pickup and backed it into the yard, right up to the wolf's cage. As she got out of the pickup, she took from the glove compartment an envelope addressed to Mr. Dolan.

"This has one copy of the notarized statement and the check. Put it in his mailbox, will you?" She let down the tailgate and took out a package of meat.

I put the letter in the empty mailbox.

"Honey, open the cage door for the rabbits, will you?"

I did, and after a minute they crept out and looked around.

"Get the hose and fill their water dish and this one for the wolf."

"Are we taking the rabbits too?"

"No, rabbits can get along. There's a whole field of veggies out there." She was murmuring to the wolf and holding a handful of meat close to her face.

"Is she alive?"

"Just barely, I'd say." She put the bowl of water near the wolf and stroked her head gently.

I was scrunched down beside the cage, but I was keeping an eye on the house too. The wolf opened her eyes and raised her head. Mom cupped her hand, scooped up some water, and held it out to her. Slowly the wolf turned her head till she could lap up the water.

"That's my girl," Mom murmured to her. She held out some meat. The wolf ate it in one gulp. Mom gave her some more and put the bowl of water close to her face.

In a few minutes the wolf was sitting up, eating in big bites.

"Lee, open the door of the carrier and put a chunk of meat in there." She handed me the water bowl. "And this." She was sounding excited. "I think we're going to have a lovely wolf."

I thought the wolf didn't look very lovely just then. She was dirty, her coat was dull and ragged, and she was about the skinniest animal I had ever seen.

I followed Mom's instructions. She coaxed the wolf to

the door of the old cage, luring her with handfuls of meat. Then very carefully she picked her up and put her in the carrier on the pickup. It scared me when she picked up the wolf. For all we knew, the wolf could be rabid. But the wolf settled down right away on the blanket Mom had put in the carrier and started to eat.

Quickly Mom closed the carrier door and put up the tailgate.

"Away we go."

We scrambled into the cab and she drove off, trying hard to avoid the worst bumps. We had just reached the road and started west when there was a sharp bang and the car swerved. For an awful minute I thought we had a flat tire, but then I saw the shattered glass of the rearview mirror on the left side of the cab, and Mom was speeding up. She reached over and shoved my head down.

"Get on the floor." She was hunkered down over the steering wheel.

I stayed on the floor, feeling all the bumps. I wanted to look back to see if the wolf was okay, but Mom shook her head when I started to raise up. She was driving fast, and the pickup was bouncing all over the road. I was afraid the poor wolf would bounce right out of the back. She must have been scared to death. I didn't think she could have been hit by a bullet though, because there had been only the one bang. If Mom hadn't had her window rolled up, she'd have gotten a faceful of flying glass.

The really scary question was, was he chasing us? There could have been a car there somewhere.

Finally I felt Mom turning onto the main road, and after a few minutes she stopped. I scrambled off the floor.

My mother was leaning her head on the steering wheel, and she was shaking.

"Mom! Are you all right?" There was a long crack in the window.

"Yes." She lifted her head. "I must have been out of my mind, taking you out there. You could have been killed."

"Me! I'm all right. I was worried about you. Did he chase us?"

"No. He just fired one shot from in front of his house. He was in there all the time, watching us. He could have shot us then." She grabbed my hand. "Whew! Wait till your father hears about this. He'll blow his top."

"Don't tell him."

"I'll tell him, but maybe I can tone it down a little. Let's see if that wolf is okay." She got out, and I jumped out on my side.

The wolf was curled up tight in a corner of the carrier. The water dish had overturned and soaked the blanket on the floor of the carrier.

"Poor baby," Mom said. "What a rescue." She stood beside the pickup, talking in a low, calm voice to the wolf, but she didn't touch anything.

We got back in the cab and headed home.

"You called her 'baby.' Is she a young wolf?"

"I'd say a yearling. Probably born a year ago last spring, maybe March or April, depending on where her mother was at the time. Temperature makes a difference. But anyway a little over a year old, I'd say."

I waited a minute before I asked what had been on my mind from the beginning. "Are we going to keep her?"

She didn't answer for ages. "I've thought about it a lot.

I guess we'll just wait and see how she does. She could die, she's in such bad shape."

"She can't die! Not after all this. I won't let her die."

"Lee, honey, be realistic. She could die. But we'll do our darndest not to let her." She turned into our dirt road, driving carefully.

CHAPTER 7

B y the time Mom had to get Savannah at the pool, we had our wolf fixed up as well as we could. First we took the carrier into the fenced-off woods, and Mom opened the door. The wolf didn't want to come out. She cowered at the back, with her ears flat.

"She may feel safer in a cage," Mom said. "She's probably spent her life in one."

"I wish I knew where her mother was," I said.

"I don't believe that man could get a pup away from its mother in the wild. She was probably born in captivity, and if she was, she wouldn't know how to look after herself in the wild."

Pretty soon Mom coaxed her to the front of the carrier by holding out a chunk of meat for her.

"She needs a den," Mom said. "Why don't you get Dad's

shovel and dig her a shallow cave back there in the woods? Pull some deadwood around the opening of the cave so it will be hidden."

I found a nice, quiet place beside a yellow jack pine, with other trees all around, and some wild huckleberry bushes. It was hard digging because I kept coming up against big tree roots, but I finally got a shallow cave dug, and I pulled branches and brush all around it.

Mom was using the damp blanket to smooth the wolf's coat and get some of the dirt off. The wolf trembled, but she didn't pull away.

"Does she swallow those big pieces of meat whole?" I said.

"Wolves have a digestive system made for tearing off chunks of meat and swallowing them whole. See those front teeth? They're sharp and pointed, not like the little incisors of animals that snap off roots and vegetation. All right, Miss Wolf, let's take you over to your den." Gently she moved her back into the carrier. "Fill a bucket from the hose and bring another hunk of meat."

When I got back with all that (and it felt yucky to pick up that raw beef in my bare hands!), the wolf had gone into her den. Mom left the meat and the water bucket just outside the den.

"Now we'll leave her alone for a while," she said.

Back at the cabin we unloaded the rest of the meat and put it in the freezer and stored the carrier in Dad's little prefab shed.

"I've got to go," Mom said. "Savannah will be waiting."

"Are you going to tell her?" I could imagine Savannah reacting one of two ways: either rushing down to the den and making a big fuss over the "sweet little wolf," or being reminded of the Doberman and having hysterics. Either way I didn't look forward to it.

"Let's wait," Mom said. "It's our secret for now. I want that wolf to have some peace and quiet."

I loved having a secret, just me and Mom and the wolf.

"What are you going to name her?"

"Think about it." She got back in the pickup and drove off.

I went inside and put a scoop of ice cream into a glass of root beer. What should we name the wolf? I thought about my favorite singers and actresses: Nanci Griffith, Meryl Streep, k. d. lang . . . none of them sounded like good names for a wolf. How about people in books? Jane for Jane Eyre? Little Nell? Dicey? Dicey wasn't bad, except it sounded chancy, and I didn't want our wolf called anything chancy.

I had another root beer as I turned on the TV and watched Dad do the noon news. He's good. He looks handsome, and he has a warm, friendly voice. I felt proud of him.

When he was finished, I began wondering what the wolf was doing. Instead of going to see, I got out my sketch pad. Mom is real good at sketching animals and plants. She illustrated a book that got published when we were in California. It was about animals and flowers and plants in Georgia. She'd worked on one in Alaska too, about animals.

I tried the outline of the wolf's head. Maybe when she got fatter and more comfortable with us, I'd do a watercolor, because she had interesting colors in her coat, even though it was so scraggly now. A coat of many colors. If she were a male, we could name her Joseph. Underneath it was gray, but on top it was different colors, white and black and kind of golden, all mixed together. Her forehead and ears were tawny, if that's the right word, and she was darker along her backbone, with a whitish kind of saddle and light-colored legs.

I was having trouble getting the shape of her head right. I'd erased it twice when I heard the pickup come in. So I put what I'd done in my desk drawer and locked it. I lock my desk drawer because Savannah has no sense of privacy.

Savannah was in the kitchen peering into the fridge. She looked cute with her blond hair still wet and curling around her face. Savannah is the family beauty, there's no argument about that. She has eyes the color of Flathead Lake the day we drove up here. And she's tall for her age, and graceful. I am short for my age, and clunky. And I have straight brown hair, cut as short as possible without making me an actual skinhead.

"I hope you left some root beer," she said.

"I did. How was the pool?" I glanced at Mom to see if she had given in and told Savannah about the wolf. She caught my eye and shook her head.

"Great," Savannah said. "We had races and I won."

"Naturally."

"Wait till Dad sees how smashed up his car got. How did that happen anyway?"

"I told you," Mom said. "Maybe a rock flew up."

"Must have been a boulder."

The trouble is, Savannah is not only pretty, she's smart. It's hard to fool her.

Mom wasn't really lying. We didn't exactly see that man shoot at us. Mom just saw him in her inside mirror, standing in front of his house, holding a gun.

Mom fixed lunch for us.

"I forgot to tell you," Savannah said, "there's a matinee movie for kids this afternoon. Disney or something. I told Annette and Billie Lee I'd meet them there."

"Have you ever heard of asking permission?" Mom said.

"Mom, I'm asking you now."

"You can go, but you'll have to ride your bike. I'm not going back to town again today."

"Oh, Mom. My legs ache from all that swimming."

"It's your choice."

Savannah argued for a minute, but she left finally on her bike. At the last possible minute she asked me if I'd like to go.

"No, thanks." Probably a cartoon movie. I could just imagine it. So much noise you couldn't think. Besides, I hoped Mom would say we could maybe go close enough to the den to make sure the wolf was okay.

And after Savannah left, that's what we did.

"I feel sneaky not telling her," Mom said, "but you know she'd want to rush right down there and pat the 'sweet little wolfie.' "

I laughed at Mom's imitation. She sounded just like Savannah.

"On the other hand," I said, "a wolf may remind her of dogs, and she's still scared of big dogs. A lot of people think wolves are scary. Maybe it's 'Little Red Riding Hood' and 'The Three Little Pigs.' "

"The wolf in 'The Three Little Pigs' was just looking for ham, pork, and bacon, like the rest of us."

We walked silently and single file through the trees. Mom pointed out some wild asparagus and some big ripe serviceberries, which we Montanans call "sarvis berries." They're delicious. I scooped up a handful.

Close to the cave, we stopped and watched. The meat Mom had left in front of the cave was gone, but we couldn't see the wolf. Not far away on the other side of a clump of trees was a small stream. It would probably dry up before the summer was over, but right now it was running along fast in a shallow little ditch. I had heard it when I was digging the den, and I'd thought it would be handy for the wolf to drink from, while it lasted.

While we stood there watching, the wolf appeared from that direction. As soon as she saw us, she froze, then lowered her head. Then she went down on her front knees.

"Why is she doing that?" I whispered.

"She's showing submission. Look at her tail."

It was low, between her hind legs, and swishing gently along the ground.

"The weaker wolves act that way with the alpha wolf, the boss. She's telling us we're the boss."

"Oh, that's awful! We don't want to be boss."

"She's been raised to submit. We'll just stay here and let her go into her den."

After a minute the wolf moved cautiously to the entrance of the den and looked at us.

"We're your friends, wolf," I said as softly as I could. "Don't feel put down."

She had really beautiful eyes, dark gold and slanted. She looked at us a moment longer and then went into the den.

"Are you going to feed her again today?" I asked. We were walking back toward the cabin.

"I think in the morning. She's been starved so long, I don't want to overfeed her. Tomorrow I'll drop in and have a talk with the vet. I noticed his place when I was bringing Savannah home."

When we were almost to the cabin, Mom said, "Have you thought of a name?"

"Not one I like."

"This may sound crazy to you, but do you remember sometimes when I used to read you Bible stories, you wanted to hear the Book of Ruth over and over?"

"I remember. She went with Naomi, her mother-in-law, to a strange land because she loved her, but she was awfully lonesome."

" 'Standing amid the alien corn.' I thought of it just now, as the wolf stood there."

"We'll call her Ruth!"

Mom smiled. "If you like it."

"I love it! My new friend Ruth. And I'll teach her not to feel lonesome."

Mom and I never told anybody why we called our wolf Ruth. It was our secret, Mom and Ruthie and me.

CHAPTER 8

Dad hit the roof when he saw the damage to his precious pickup.

"I knew he'd be mad," Savannah said, enjoying every minute of it.

"Calm down, Paul," Mom said. "The insurance will cover it. I'll take it into Kalispell tomorrow and get it fixed. You can use my car."

"I don't like your car. It's too small."

I tried not to laugh. My father is only five foot nine. He has this picture of himself, I guess, as John Wayne in those old western movies. I've noticed how a lot of western men seem to think of a pickup as a substitute for the horse they don't have anymore. You can ride across range country in a pickup, and maybe it's the next best thing to a horse.

"What I can't figure," Dad was saying, "is how that mirror got broken up so bad that it cracked the window too."

"Look," Mom said, and I knew by the glance she threw at me that she was about to tell all. "Come out and let's take a look at the pickup. I want to talk to you."

"I've seen it." He was opening his one beer a night.

"I know you've seen it. I want to talk to you." She sounded exasperated enough so that he paid attention. The two of them went outside.

"It wasn't really a rock," Savannah said to me, "and you might as well tell me. Mom is telling Dad, and I'm not going to be the only one left out."

"All right, but I'm setting down the conditions, and you have to swear to stick by them."

"Since when did you get to be the big honcho?"

"Since you want to know about the pickup."

She thought it over. One thing about my sister, if she makes a serious promise and remembers that she made it, she'll keep it.

"All right. I promise."

So I told her the whole story, and she didn't interrupt me once. Her eyes got bigger and bigger. Right at the end she burst into tears.

I thought it was the part about Mom and me getting shot at.

"He probably didn't even mean to hit us," I said. "He must be a real good shot to place it right where it would scare us, maybe make us run off the road. We came near it."

But it wasn't the danger to Mom and me she was crying

about. "I'm terrified of wolves," she said. "I can't even look at them on the Nature Channel. Those fangs!"

I was shocked that it wasn't us she worried about. "They just have those fangs for eating meat. They have to tear it off the deer and caribou."

She gave a small scream. "He'll tear my flesh right off my bones."

I was getting disgusted. "It's a she, and wolves only eat animals with hooves. You don't have any hooves."

"Who's going to stop to look?"

I couldn't help laughing. I got this mental picture of a hungry wolf stopping somebody and saying, "Excuse me, do you mind if I check the bottoms of your feet?"

"It's not funny." She was mad now. She mopped her face with her sleeve. "I'm not living with any wolf. Dad will get rid of it. I'll make him."

That made me mad. "Number one, don't think you can tell Dad what to do."

"I can persuade him. Every time."

"Number two, it's our wolf, Mom's and mine, not Dad's or yours."

"Yuck! You bet it isn't mine. But Dad is the boss."

"You've got to be kidding."

"Well, he wanted to move here and Mom didn't, but here we are, and it's Dad's place."

"It's Mom's house." This was getting silly, but I couldn't let her get away with thinking she ran the family.

"It is not. It's our house."

"If you want to know the facts, ma'am, Nonny paid for it, and the deed is in Mom's name, and it comes to you and me when Mom dies. That was the deal."

"How soon am I dying?" It was Mom coming in the door.

I was embarrassed, especially since we hadn't meant to tell Savannah yet. "We were just having a hypothetical discussion."

"Does Savannah always cry during hypothetical discussions?"

I thought I might as well get it over with. "I told her the whole story, about Ruthie."

"Ruthie!" Savannah exploded. "Ruthie who?"

"Well, I told your dad," Mom said, "and he's so mad, he's out there reading the riot act to that woodpecker that's been waking us up every morning." She began to laugh. "He washes his hands of the whole affair, which is fine with me."

"And we don't have to worry about Savannah bothering Ruthie. She's terrified of wolves."

Savannah began to cry again, and I felt guilty.

"Look, Sis," I said, "this is a little old half-starved wolf who's a lot scareder of any of us than we are of her. She's living in a den way down in the woods, and you don't even have to see her."

"It'll come in the night and get us." Sob.

Mom put her arm around Savannah. "Darling, I can show you book after book about wolves that say wolves are gentle animals, and they have never in the whole history of this country been known to attack a human being. They don't think we taste good."

I decided to leave it to Mom. I went outside, avoiding Dad, who was leaning against his pickup, staring at the broken mirror as if the whole truck was a mass of tangled metal. I let myself in through the gate and walked through the trees toward the den.

It was hot in the woods, and mosquitoes and midges swarmed around my face. I swatted one mosquito on my arm and drew blood. Only pregnant female mosquitoes bite, so I guess I just wiped out the next generation.

Ruthie was sitting outside her den. She pulled back closer to the entrance as I came toward her. I sat down without getting too close.

"Ruthie," I said, "if you could hear the hullabaloo that's going on up at the cabin, you wouldn't feel shy. According to popular opinion, you are a savage, dangerous, ravening beast who's laying plans right now to tear great chunks off our bodies while we sleep."

She had her head tucked down, the way she does.

"If you knew the state my sister is in, you'd hold your head up and probably laugh right out loud. It *is* kind of funny, you and Savannah both scared to death of each other."

Even with her head down, I could see her eyes. They were very expressive. Today the expression looked to me like a combination of fear and curiosity. She wasn't used to somebody sitting on the ground and talking to her. I tried to remember not to stare into her eyes, because Mom said all animals take that as a sign of aggression, even dogs if they don't know you. It was hard not to watch her though. I kept talking.

"When you feel more secure, I'm going to come out here and sketch you. I have this crazy idea, maybe I could do a picture book someday, with the story of how you came to live with us."

She backed partway into the cave, as if she had understood me and did not wish to be a heroine in a book, thank you. I laughed.

"We'll give you a fake name so you can stay anonymous. We could call you Lupe, Queen of the Forest. Lupus is the word for the species dogs come from, so it probably includes you too. You know these things when your mom is a biologist. Lupe, Queen of the Forest. It has a nice sound."

She disappeared into the den.

That night Savannah kept her bedside lamp on to protect her from wolves.

CHAPTER 9

Savannah tried to cope with her fear of Ruthie by pretending she wasn't there. "She's probably run away by now," she said, although she knew perfectly well that I was going down to the den every day to feed her and spend a little time talking to her.

A couple of times Savannah woke up screaming in the middle of the night, saying she had heard wolves outside her window.

Dad always investigated, going out in his pajamas with his flashlight, to reassure her. Once it was a deer, who looked him over and then leaped off into the dark. The second time he came into the house in a hurry, and we could smell the reason why. But the skunk had missed him.

"Vannie," he kept telling my sister, "the wolf is fenced

in. She couldn't get to the cabin even if she wanted to, and it's the last thing a wolf would do."

I got exasperated, but I felt sorry for her too because I think the fear was real. She was pretty small when the Doberman bit her, and he really hurt her. She had blood gushing out of her arm, and it took several stitches to sew it up. But then there's always the actress in Savannah who plays everything up. It's hard to tell the fake from the real sometimes.

She went into town most days, always with a pack of friends around her. Somehow she wangled a nonpaying job taking posters around town for the summer theater. And of course she hung around there a lot. They gave her free tickets for delivering the posters. She told Nonny she was practically a member of the cast.

A couple of times I went swimming late in the day, when the crowd thinned out. I had sort of a thing for the lifeguard. His name was Bryan, and he told me he was half Hawaiian. But you weren't supposed to talk to the lifeguard, and he was pretty busy hauling little kids out of deep water and yelling at boys who thought it was fun to push a girl underwater. I half drowned a jerk named Donny who tried it on me.

I spent a lot of time sketching Ruthie. When Mom realized what I was doing, she got me a new sketch pad and drawing pencils, and gave me advice when I asked for it.

Ruthie was still shy, but I talked to her a lot, and she sat with her head on one side, listening. I wished I could read her mind.

One day about a week after we got her, I was home alone. Mom had gone to Kalispell. She was being interviewed by the community college for a fall teaching job, and also she was signing up with the school district for subbing.

The phone rang. A strange woman's voice said, "Hello? Is this Anita McDougall?"

Right away I was thinking that something had happened to Savannah.

"Who is this?" I said. "What's happened?"

"This is the Montana Bank in Missoula. Am I speaking to Mrs. McDougall?"

I nearly fell over with relief—just a bank. "She's not here right now. Can I help you?"

"Are you her daughter?"

I said I was, and I gave her my name.

"Well, we've had a slight problem. I just wanted to ask her a question. A man came in here yesterday at closing time and wanted to cash a check signed by your mother. He didn't have any ID, and he wouldn't wait while we called your house for verification. In fact, he got quite abusive. I suppose he'll be back, so I thought we'd better check on it."

"Is his name A. Dolan, and is the check for fifty dollars?"

"Yes." She sounded relieved. "Your mother did give an A. Dolan a check? Do you happen to know what this man looks like?"

"He looks like a drunken bum."

She laughed. "The description fits."

"He's not a friend or anything," I said. "My mother

bought an animal from him. He's kind of tall and stooped and skinny, with about three strands of gray hair, and he needs a shave."

"That's our man. How old are you, Lee, if I may ask?"

"Thirteen." Did she think I was six or something?

"When your mother has time, perhaps she'd give me a collect call." She gave me the number. "I'm sure it's this Dolan. Your description is very good. But just for the record."

"Sure, I'll tell her."

"Many thanks. Have a nice day."

I wrote Mom a note, so I wouldn't forget.

She got home about four o'clock. By the time we got the groceries unpacked, she decided she'd call the woman in the morning.

"Banks close early, don't they?" She looked tired.

I was stacking big chunks of raw meat in the freezer for Ruthie when I heard a car drive in. It was too early for Dad. I finished what I was doing and came in the back door in time to hear Mom saying in a funny strained voice, "As long as you're sure it's nothing to do with my daughter or my husband . . . ?"

A deep voice said, "No, no, ma'am, nothing to disturb you at all. I'm just checking out a bit of information."

"Well, come into the kitchen and have a cup of coffee. I've been shopping."

I was washing my hands when they came into the kitchen. I nearly fainted when I saw him. He was a cop, and he looked about ten feet tall.

"This is my daughter Lee," Mom said, "and you are Officer . . . ?"

"McLaren." He shook hands with me, and I felt swallowed up. "Well," he said, "the McDougalls and the Mc-Larens. That calls for bagpipes." He sat down on one of our kitchen chairs and it creaked.

Mom was pouring coffee from the Krups. "Cream and sugar, Officer McLaren?"

"Please, ma'am."

Officer McLaren took a long swallow of very hot coffee. "I just wanted to ask you if you knew anybody named A. Dolan."

"Oh, that." Mom looked relieved. "The bank called while I was out, about the check. Apparently he had no ID, but it's a good check. Fifty dollars. I bought an animal from him that he was not taking proper care of."

He raised his bushy eyebrows. "For fifty dollars? Pedigreed dog or something?"

Mom looked a little annoyed. I did too. What business was it of his?"

"No," she said, "not a pedigreed dog."

"I see."

I was leaning against the sink. He'd found out what he wanted to know, and he'd drained off the coffee in about three swallows, so why didn't he leave?

"I'll call the bank in the morning," Mom said.

"That won't be necessary."

"Oh? You'll notify them then." When he didn't answer, she said, "Do they always call in the police for such a small matter?"

He leaned back in the chair, and I waited for it to crack.

"Well, the truth is, ma'am, it's not all that small a matter. This A. Dolan was found in the parking lot in back of a bar in Missoula early this morning, and the only ID on him was your check."

Mom looked startled. "Found?"

"He was dead. Shot through the chest."

CHAPTER 10

Mom got a Coke and put it in my hand. "Sit down, honey," she said. "You look pale."

I slid down with my back against the sink until I was sitting on the floor. I felt like puking. Mom didn't look too great either.

"Who killed him?" she said. "And what on earth for? The man had nothing."

"Except your check, and two dollars and forty-five cents." He put two heaping spoonfuls of sugar in his second cup of coffee. "Seems he and another fella were in this bar down by the railroad tracks, both of 'em drunk as skunks. They got into a noisy argument and the bartender threw 'em out. Apparently they kept on arguing out back in the parking lot, and the other guy shot him. That's the story. No proof yet. They've got the other fella in for questioning."

"Why didn't somebody hear the shot? Or did they?"

He shook his head. "Noisy part of town. Trains and all."

"About what time was this?"

"They left the bar a little after midnight, bartender says."

Mom thought a moment. "No trains through there then."

He gave her a funny look. "Now how would you know that, ma'am?"

"I was a train dispatcher." She snapped it at him, and then said, "Sorry, it's rather shocking to hear somebody you just talked to has been murdered."

He shrugged. "It happens with that kind of guy." He spread out a notebook on the table. "Missoula wants to know a little more about this guy. You say you went to his place. Can you tell me where it was?"

"I'd better tell you the whole story." Mom went into the other room and brought back the second copy of the notarized paper.

"Mr. Dolan had a copy of this." Then she told the cop all about the zoo and Ruthie and how we took her and left the money and the paper, and how he shot out the rearview mirror.

He wrote it all down. "You'd done better, I guess, just to tell the Humane Society about this wolf."

"They'd have to put her down." It was the first thing I'd said.

He shrugged. "So you're stuck with an unhealthy animal. Could be trouble."

"She's not unhealthy," I said. "She was just hungry. She's getting better every day."

He pushed back his chair and stood up. "Some ranchers around here don't take too kindly to wolves."

"She's fenced in," Mom said.

He smiled at me. "I bet you named her already." I nodded. "That's what my kids would do," he said. "My youngest's got a pet spider in a bottle, calls her Priscilla. I ask you! Where'd she hear a name like that?" He put his notepad in his pocket. "Just remember, young lady, a wolf ain't a dog."

"It is, though," I said. "If you look at a diagram of their evolution, the wolf and the dog didn't branch off from each other till about fifteen thousand years ago."

"No kidding!" He winked at my mother. "Practically kissing cousins."

I said "smart ass!" under my breath, but by then he and Mom were in the living room and couldn't hear me.

When Mom came back, we talked about A. Dolan.

"If I hadn't seen that zoo sign," I said, "I guess he'd still be alive."

"Or I could say if I hadn't taken the wolf away and left him a check that took him to Missoula. No, that won't do. Every action we ever take has consequences, and we don't know what they'll be. If the action is made in good faith, then we are not to blame for what follows."

"I don't suppose he had a real swinging life anyway," I said.

"No, but I doubt that he'd have asked to be shot in the chest. Well, enough of this. I'd better get dinner started. You want to wash some lettuce for me?"

I washed lettuce and defrocked ears of corn and sliced the tails off radishes and thought about A. Dolan, and who is responsible for what, and how do you know?

CHAPTER 11

My father's reaction to the whole A. Dolan story was the last thing I expected.

"Terrific!" he said. "Woman and child save starving wolf from brutal owner, get shot at and almost killed, man goes to Missoula to cash his ill-gotten check and gets murdered in back of a bar. Wait till I give the boss this story, on a golden platter!"

"What are you talking about?" Mom looked horrified. "The last thing we want is publicity. It's a grim, tragic story, Paul."

"Of course it is. Just what they love. And if you think it's going to stay a secret, you don't know the American press. It'll be headlined in the *Missoulian* tomorrow, and on every radio station. But we can scoop 'em." He went for the telephone. "We'll get you and Lee on the air to tell the story before it breaks anywhere. Wolves are big news right now."

Savannah was listening with wide eyes. I could see the wheels spinning in her head. "What a break!" she said.

Dad was dialing the station. "It won't hurt me to bring the boss a scoop like this! In a new job every little thing counts."

Mom clamped her hand on the phone. "Paul, we are not going anywhere near TV. We don't want to publicize this wolf."

"Honey, this is a break for me. I won't interview you myself; that wouldn't look good. But Dan can do it. He's fine at interviews." He pulled away from her and began dialing again. "The story's got everything. It's just the kind of yarn about Montana that people love. Wouldn't surprise me if it hit 'All Things Considered,' maybe *USA Today*." On the phone he said, "Joan? Paul McDougall here. Has the big man gone home? . . . oh, nuts. Well, I'll catch him there. Thanks, honey." He hung up. "I'd better call Joe too. We'll need shots of the wolf before it gets too dark."

This time I grabbed him. "You're not taking any pictures of my wolf." I could imagine Ruthie, strangers swarming around her den, noise, flashbulbs going off. It would undo all the progress we'd made, which wasn't much but was a start.

"Let go, Lee." He pushed me away.

"Stop this!" Mom's voice stopped us all in our tracks. "We are not going on TV or radio and we are not talking to the press. Neither of us, and nobody is going near the wolf."

Dad got red in the face. His nose twitched. "We are talking about my job here. This could make my career."

"I'm sorry," Mom said. "You'll have to make it some other way."

His fists were clenched. "This is my house and my job, and if I say do it, we'll do it."

There was a pause that you could hear clear to California. Then Mom said, "I don't like to point this out, I really don't, but the house is not yours."

"The land is mine." He sounded choked.

"The wolf is not yours."

I was shaking. They often had fights, but this one was kind of scary.

Then Savannah moved into the scene. "Not to worry," she said, in her new star-of-the-season voice. "There's no need to take pictures of the wolf. You can find a stock shot of some scraggly-looking wolf in the files at the station. And Mom and Lee don't need to be bothered. I'll do the interview."

Silence. Very different thoughts were going through different heads: Me: outrage. Mom: dismay. Dad: slowly arriving at "Hey, why not?"

"You've never even seen Ruthie," I said. "You never saw the zoo. You never saw Mr. Dolan."

"So what?" She was glowing like one of those Fourth of July candles. "I'm an actress, aren't I? Do you think Nonny saw Joan of Arc before she played her?"

"Why not!" Now Dad was jubilant. "Go get into your best bib and tucker, fast. Something girlish, not too sophisticated. The fresh-faced Montana girl . . . Hurry!" He was dialing as Savannah dashed for her room. "They'll do the makeup at the studio," he called after her.

"Paul," my mother began.

But he was already talking on the phone. "John? Paul here. Listen, man, I've got the story of the year for you. We have to get on it fast, beat out Missoula. . . . Yeah, one starving wolf, one woman and child who risk their lives to save wolf, get shot at by maniac zookeeper, who they've already paid for the wolf, all legit. Man goes to Missoula to cash check, gets murdered in drunken brawl. Is that local color or is that local color? . . . No, they're shook up, but my younger daughter is going to do it. She's a born actress. Her grandmom is Savannah Saxton, don't forget. . . . Yeah, her name is Savannah too. That part won't hurt. . . . Righto. Oh, and John, I get credit, right? On my dossier, I mean." He gave his boss a chuckle. "See you there."

Mom and I stood there and watched as Dad and Savannah got their act together and went roaring off in Mom's car.

"We should have stopped them," I said. I felt sick.

"Except he's right, it will be in the media."

"What we have to do," I said, "is get a padlock for that gate."

"We'll have the fence electrified. I'll do it in the morning."

"Mom," I said, "can you believe this?"

"Oh, yes," Mom said. "I grew up with one Savannah Saxton. Now I'm growing old with another one."

I started to cry. "She'll ruin everything. They'll take Ruthie away."

"Over my dead body. I bought and paid for that wolf, and nobody's going to take her away."

"She'll say Ruthie is vicious."

"I don't think she will, honey. Van isn't that mean. I don't really think she's mean at all. She's just so concentrated on herself." She hugged me. "Don't worry. Would you like some dinner?"

"I'm not hungry."

"Well, we'd better turn on the TV and wait for the star. Why don't you put a blank tape in the VCR? Nonny will never forgive us if we don't capture this immortal moment for her."

"Okay." I mopped my face with my sleeve and went to look for a tape.

"It will probably come on at the end of the local news. How about if I make us some popcorn?"

So we sat there and watched the news: car wreck near Whitefish, one man killed; governor vetoes legislature's special-session budget; trout scarce this year in the Blackfoot.

"And *now*," said my dad's associate, whom he calls Dapper Dan, "we have a special report."

The camera zoomed in on Miss Savannah Saxton McDougall, sitting at her ease at a small table, smiling graciously, as if she got interviewed on TV every day.

I closed my eyes tight.

CHAPTER 12

As they used to say in the old Hollywood gossip columns," Mom said, "she never looked lovelier."

Dapper Dan was feeding her questions. She did look beautiful, and about sixteen years old. And she never missed a beat.

Yes, it was true that her mother had just bought an abused wolf from Mr. A. Dolan. Yes, he did have a so-called zoo just south of Bigfork.

"What was this place like, Miss McDougall? May I call you Savannah?"

"Please do," said Miss McDougall. "I'm rather proud of the name. I'm named for my grandmother, Savannah Saxton."

"Oh, of course." You could tell Dapper Dan had never

heard of Nonny. "What was this zoo place like, Savannah?"

She never said she hadn't seen the place herself. She described it the way Mom and I had told it, as if she had been there. She described A. Dolan right down to the wisps of gray hair.

"And your heart went out to this poor neglected wolf."

"Oh, yes." Savannah Saxton McDougall registered pain. "I love animals. I can't stand to see them abused. He was so pathetic."

I looked at Mom. "He?"

Dan led her into the whole story about our going back and giving Mr. Dolan the check and the "bill of sale."

"She's goofing up," I said.

"No, I think Dad wants it to look like a regular sale. Nothing about leaving the check in the mailbox," Mom said.

"And this man shot at your car when you were driving away?"

How would she deal with that? A guy doesn't shoot you for giving him fifty bucks. Answer that one, Miss Savannah!

"Obviously the man was mentally disturbed," she said serenely.

Dapper Dan told us avid listeners how A. Dolan had been found murdered in a parking lot behind a bar in Missoula.

"And the only ID was your mother's check?"

"Yes. The bank had called my mother before, because he tried to cash the check without any ID. But she wasn't home when they called. I told the bank teller the circumstances, but Mr. Dolan had already left in a towering rage."

"So you have the wolf, Savannah, and are you going to make a pet of him?"

"Oh no. We'll just keep him till he's healthy enough to be set free."

I yelled.

Mom shook her head. "Cool it. That's a good answer. People won't come hanging around here to see the wolf if they think she's been set free."

"But she means it. She wants to get rid of Ruthie."

"One last question," Dapper Dan was saying. "If you'll forgive my asking, how old are you, Savannah?"

"Fourteen," she said, and gave him her most gracious smile.

"Hah!" I said. "Wait till she shows up in the sixth grade next fall!"

The camera cut back to the announcer, and Mom clicked off the TV and the VCR. "Your grandmother will be thrilled."

"Mom, Ruthie is my wolf. Savannah's trying to take her away from me. She's trying to take my *life* away from me."

"Actors tend to do that. I mean that's what it's all about. But if I know you, Lee, nobody will ever take your life away from you. Or your wolf either."

"Do you know where the flashlight is?"

"In the top desk drawer. Why?"

"I want to go see Ruthie for a minute."

Ruthie was sitting outside her den, looking at the moon. She pricked her ears forward when she saw me. I had the feeling for a second that she was glad to see me.

I told her the whole story. "I guess it's the difference between art and a pack of lies. Savannah thinks she gave a performance. Nonny will think so too. To me she's trying to grab the spotlight, grabbing an important piece of my life and making it sound like it's hers. I think that's a pack of lies. Well, it's a lucky thing for me she's scared to death of you, or she'd be down here trying to get you to like her best. I don't know if you like me at all, Ruthie, but I like you a whole lot. And nobody, but nobody, is going to take you away or bother you or, if I can help it, even see you. And Mom's on my side."

We sat there quietly for a little while. The moon was almost full, and the moonlight spilled through the spaces in the trees like something soft you could touch. There were all those little night sounds you hear in the forest, and you can't tell what they are, but you know there are a lot of living things all around you. It calmed me down to sit there. Savannah would never know about this; she wouldn't even feel it.

"It's not that I don't love my sister," I said. "It's just that sometimes I'd like to kill her."

CHAPTER 13

For two days I didn't talk to my sister. She couldn't understand that. Everybody else was telling her how wonderful she was—except Mom, who followed a middle path. She tried to make Savannah understand that she had picked up my story and run with it.

"She could have gone on the show herself," Savannah said. (She was referring to it as "the show" now.)

So the first thing I said to her after two days of silence was, "You called Ruthie 'he.' "

She shrugged. "He, she. Who cares?"

"How would you like it if people referred to you as he?"

She laughed. "They never would."

She had a point there.

The story of A. Dolan and the wolf did not make waves, however. There was nothing except a paragraph on page 2 of the *Missoulian* and a couple of sentences on KUFM local news. Savannah had hoped for a headline and picture in *USA Today*.

For a few days her friends at the pool made her a hero and wanted to come see the wolf. I heard her telling them that "he" was not safe to approach. "He's a wild animal, after all."

Poor little Ruthie. I worried about her, though. So many more people knew about her now. And there were people out there who hated wolves.

When the video got to Nonny, Savannah got a chance to replay the story, with embellishments, on the phone. However, Mom set Nonny straight on whose wolf it was, and what had really happened.

I could hear Nonny laugh. She has an actor's voice that reaches, as she always says, "to the second balcony." I don't think theaters have second balconies anymore, but never mind. I could hear her.

"You know, darling," Nonny was saying, "not for nothing is the child named Savannah."

"I know, Mother. I'm more aware of it every day."

Nonny's laugh again. "Don't sound so desperate, love. If she gets too much for you, send her to me."

"I may do that."

Then Nonny talked to me awhile. I have to say she gives me my fair share of attention. She's always interested in my drawing and whatever else I'm into. This time she asked about the wolf.

"Does the creature bite?" She had Mom back on the line now.

"Of course not, Mother. Wolves don't bite people. The biggest problem is curious people wandering out here to see her, see the wolf, I mean. My long-suffering husband had to put up a gate on the road at the edge of our property, and I hung a couple of signs on it: PRIVATE PROPERTY, NO TRESPASSING. That kind of thing. Not that the gate would keep anyone out who wanted to get in, and it is a nuisance whenever we drive in or out. But we can't have strangers hanging around. They never get a look at the wolf anyway. She's too shy."

"It all sounds very dramatic," Nonny said. "Have a lovely summer, darling." And she was gone.

"Nonny is like summer lightning," I said.

"That's a good line. Write it down."

"Was it hard being her child?"

Mom thought a minute. "It was different. Ups and downs."

Mom went to work on her garden, and I went out to see Ruthie. She was just coming back from the stream. Her coat was still ragged because it was that time of year, summer, but it didn't look so dull, and she was no longer a bag of bones.

She wasn't scared of me anymore either, although she still wouldn't let me come too close. She went over to the den and sat down, her ears perked up, and looked at me as if to say, "What's new?"

I lay down on my back and looked up at the sky. "Let me tell you the story of evolution," I said to Ruthie. "Let me tell you how human beings evolved from the lower species and became so wonderful and kind and good and smart, you wouldn't believe it."

She lay down and put her head on her paws, watching me.

"No," I said, "you wouldn't believe it."

CHAPTER 14

On my fourteenth birthday my mother gave me a computer. I couldn't believe it. I'd been working on my story about Ruthie, using a spiral notebook, and I guess she'd noticed. Mrs. Poole at the school in Missoula said I had a "gift," but I'd had no idea how hard it was to write a real story. I rewrote more than I wrote. I'd learned to use a computer in Germany; it would be a big help.

"You never gave me a word processor," Savannah said.

"You don't process words," Mom said.

"I thought Lee drew things."

"You can draw things on a computer if you really want to. But in fact I gave it to Lee because I think my younger child is going to be an actress and my older child is going to be a writer. Fair enough?"

Her face lit up. "Hey, Lee, you can write me a starring vehicle!"

Dad gave me a good camera and took us to Missoula, where we picked up Holly and her mom and had dinner at the Edgewater Inn. It was very nice, and Savannah forgot to feel neglected. In fact she gave me a present that really touched me. It was a tiny crystal locket shaped like a snowflake that Nonny had given her years ago. I'd always wished it was mine. I knew she loved it too, though; it wasn't a case of palming something off on me that she didn't want anyway.

"From actress to actress to artist," she had written on the card in her neat script. "Wear it in good health. Love, Van."

I started to give her a hug, something I hadn't done since she was little, but she backed off with a kidding-dramatic gesture. "No, no, not that, she cried in accents wild." And we all broke up. It was a line from our childhood that Nonny used to say, making fun of a melodramatic part she'd had in a B movie once.

"This is the nicest birthday I ever had," I told my family when we got home.

"All this and Wolfie too," Savannah said.

I looked at her, her tanned face and sun-streaked hair, the slender, graceful body, and that voice, not like an eleven-year-old voice at all, and I thought, She really will be a good actress. She's got what it takes, including knowing how to stand off and look at people objectively. A writer ought to do that too. I'd better start working on it.

The next day, Day One of my fifteenth year on this

planet, something happened that shook the world. My world anyway.

Mom and Savannah had gone into town, and I was fooling around with my computer. It was a brand I wasn't used to. And I was thinking hard about my story, the one I wanted to write about Ruthie. I couldn't get a handle on it. I didn't know how to work in A. Dolan without making it too gross for young kids. But without him, I wouldn't have any conflict, and I had heard a million times from Nonny that a story has to have conflict. Maybe I'd have to forget the real story and make up my own details.

The phone rang. A man's voice said, "Is this the McDougall residence?"

"Yes," I said, expecting some supersalesman, "but the lady of the house has gone to Outer Mongolia, and we don't want any." I started to hang up, but the guy laughed, so I hung on to hear what the joke was.

"I'll bet you're Savannah," he said.

"I'll bet you're wrong." Then it occurred to me it might be the theater people offering her a walk-on or whatever it was she was forever dreaming of. "Savannah isn't here. Can I give her a message?"

"If I'm not being too rude, who are you?"

"Savannah's sister."

"And your mom's not home either, right?"

"Right."

"Then I'll have to talk to you."

"I guess it's just not your lucky day."

"No, no, I didn't mean it that way. I have a problem, and I haven't got much time. Please excuse me, but how old are you?"

"I'm fourteen, not that it's anyone's business." I was getting annoyed.

"You're quite right, but let me explain. I live on a place up north of Columbia Falls, but I have to go away, very urgent business."

Since he paused, I said, "Well, have a nice trip."

"Miss McDougall, stop smarting off a minute and let me explain. I've been living up here for five years, and I have four wolves."

"You *what*?"

"Yes, I thought you'd be interested. I saw your sister on TV, and I read the story in the paper about the wolf she saved."

I let that go. "What about your wolves?"

"I don't know what to do with them. There's an alpha male and a female. . . . 'Alpha' means boss."

"I know that. What about them?"

"And a yearling and a pup that's five months old. My urgent problem, Miss McDougall, is what am I going to do with them?"

I didn't even stop to think. "Bring them here."

"Ah! I hoped you'd say that! Do you have room?"

"We've got acres and acres of woods, fenced in. Electric fence."

"Perfect! But what will your parents say?"

I hadn't stopped to think of that. Well, live dangerously. "They'll be delighted." I was pretty sure Mom would be, and I knew Dad would not. As for Savannah . . . don't even think about it.

"I have to catch an early morning plane," he said. "Can I bring them now?"

71

"Why not?"

"Great! What a load off my mind. They're terrific animals, really. I found the two when they were very young. Their mother had been shot. So I raised them. The female had one pup each year. I'll be there in half an hour."

I hung up and realized I didn't even know his name.

I ran through the forest to Ruthie's den. She was lying down in a clump of chokecherry bushes, gnawing on a bone. She'd gotten so she didn't sidle back to her den when I came.

"Ruthie! Big news! You're going to have four playmates! Hey, you're going to love it—" I stopped. "Or are you?" I hadn't even thought how it might affect her. "Listen," I said, and now I was starting to feel uneasy. "No matter what, always remember you are my number-one wolf. No matter how many alphas or yearlings or pups, Ruthie is top wolf."

She gave me a long, serious look. I began to worry.

CHAPTER 15

I went out to the road to watch for the man and his wolves. How would he ever find us? I should have given him directions. He hadn't even told me his name.

After what seemed like years, and no wolves, I went back to the cabin and sat on the steps. By that time I was a nervous wreck, scared that he wouldn't come, scared that he would.

I thought if I could get to Mom first, she'd be pleased. She'd probably think of a biological study to do right away. With some of her beautiful sketches. Maybe she'd do a book on raising wolves in captivity. The pup would make a perfect study.

On the other hand, maybe she'd be furious, me making a major decision like that on my own, not even asking the guy to wait till she got home so he could talk to her. But he said he couldn't wait. What was his big rush anyway? Maybe he was escaping the law. Maybe I was aiding and abetting a criminal.

And Dad. Dad was going to be really, really mad. Not that he didn't like animals—but a total of five wolves? First thing he'd say would be, "Who's going to pay the feed bill?"

And Savannah of course would have screaming hysterics. She could sort of forget about Ruthie, since she never saw her, but these new wolves were a pack. They weren't scared little orphans like Ruthie. They'd be wandering around the woods in full sight.

I went inside to look at the clock. He'd been forty-five minutes already. Maybe it was a joke. Dad had a co-worker at the station who liked to do practical jokes. Maybe it was him.

Be calm, I told myself. Get a book. Get a Coke. Sit on the steps and be nonchalant, so if he comes, or if the practical joker shows up, it'll look as if the whole thing has slipped your mind. What wolves? Oh, *those* wolves. Right. Just put them in the woods and remember to close the gate when you come out. Have a nice day.

I saw that the Coke I thought I'd opened was one of Savannah's revolting grape drinks. I poured the rest of it on the ground.

I heard a car. It stopped, and I heard the slight squeak of the new gate being opened. I should have thought to open it myself. Oh, well. I dropped my book and picked it up again fast before it got grape-frosted dirt on it. The car was too noisy for Mom's and moving too slowly to be Dad's. My stomach went into granny knots. I was sweating cannonballs.

I saw the front end of a Scout. As it moved closer, I saw that it was pulling a trailer with a tarp over it like a circus tent. The trailer said U-Haul. The driver stopped and stuck his head out. He looked like Garth Brooks, only older.

"McDougall?"

I nodded. My mouth was too dry to speak.

He did some fancy maneuvering until he was backing the trailer into our yard, right up to the fence where Ruthie was—or would have been if she hadn't melted into the forest when she heard the car.

He jumped out and grinned. "Sorry I'm late. I took the wrong turn and almost got my head shot off by your friendly neighbor." He held out his hand. "Arthur Washington."

"Lee McDougall," I said. "Did he know you had wolves?"

"Unfortunately they did a little barking. Yes, he doesn't care for wolves, it seems." He took the tarp off the trailer.

I thought I was going to faint. The four most beautiful wolves I had ever seen were standing there looking at me! Like Ruthie's, their coats were a bit ragged at this time of year, but these wolves were gorgeous. And they were mine!

"What do you think?" He looked anxious, as if I might say, "Sorry, wrong size" or "The color doesn't match my decor."

I swallowed. "Nice wolves."

He laughed. "I like a woman of few words. So is it okay if I let the wolves out? They'll make themselves at home."

I nodded.

"Where's your wolf?"

"Probably hiding in her den." Poor Ruthie. How was she going to cope with this beauty parade?

"She'll get used to them. Though they probably won't ever take her into the bosom of the family. Wolves are clannish."

"They won't hurt her, will they?"

"Oh, no. Just ignore her a bit." He was petting the wolves, stroking their heads. The big one, who had to be the alpha male, was dark, but his chest, front legs, and the lower part of his face were white. He had blue eyes. The other wolves were huddled close to him.

"Which one is the pup?"

He pointed to one that was almost white. "He's nearly as big as the yearling now." Gently he urged them out of the trailer into the woods. They kept close together, the alpha in the lead, peering around.

"Have they got names?"

"Yes, but you can rename them if you want. They won't care." He put up the tailgate of the trailer, got in the car and pulled forward a little, then got out and carefully latched the gate. Turning to me, he took a long envelope out of his hip pocket. He was wearing designer jeans, I noticed now, and the kind of shirt my father makes fun of but really would like to have, very good cotton and button-down collar. "You probably wonder if I'm on the lam, doing all this in such a hurry. I am, in a way. My estranged wife just found out how much I'm getting for an advance on my new book, and she doesn't want to be estranged anymore."

"Oh. But *you* do?"

"Yes. I am fleeing like a craven coward. I am leaving her the place, lock, stock, and barrel, but not the wolves and not me." He opened the fat envelope and made a note on a piece of paper. "All you need to know is here. Rabies shots, names and ages, the works." He gave my hand a firm shake. "Take good care of them, Lee. They're the best friends I ever had. If you ever come to Europe, look me up." He gave me that big grin, got into his car, made a careful turn, and was gone, the trailer rattling and bumping behind him.

When I turned back to look at the wolves, they had disappeared, just melted into the woods. I decided to leave them alone till they got used to the place. I was sure Ruthie would be in her den, trying to figure out what was happening. I wondered whether I should introduce them, make sure they didn't get rough or scare her, but he had said they wouldn't. It might cause more trouble if I mixed up in it.

I went into the cabin, feeling dazed. I had a wolf pack. Five wolves. It was either the most wonderful or the most disastrous thing I'd ever gotten into.

CHAPTER 16

I tried to think. There ought to be something I should be doing besides standing in the middle of the kitchen. He must have fed them. I'd better check the locker to see if we had enough for everybody for supper.

Water. I filled two buckets with water at the hose connection outside and carried them to the gate.

The wolves were nowhere in sight, but I knew they were probably watching me. I set down the buckets inside the fence, and waited outside. In a few minutes one of them came out. Then another. Another and another, all coming from slightly different directions, as if they had been standing back there waiting to see what happened next.

It was eerie how silent they were. And so beautiful. We'd have to think of names for them. I'd let Savannah name the first one so she wouldn't feel so scared of them.

If you name something, it becomes partly you, doesn't it?

The yearling was a lot bigger and heavier than Ruthie, but of course he was a male, and he'd been well taken care of. I wished I could go get her.

As I watched, they came over to the water buckets. The others stood back while the alpha male sampled the water. He was a big guy, with powerful legs and chest. I was glad I knew wolves were friendly.

When he finished drinking, the female—she was the only female—moved in; the yearling went up to the other bucket, and the pup pushed against his mother to get his nose in. She moved over for him. They drank a lot.

I went back to the gate and went in, slowly, and just stood there and let them make the next move. The yearling was the first. He came to me carefully, ready to run off if I made a wrong gesture. I held out my hand. He backed off, then came in again and sniffed it right up my arm. It was a weird feeling. His nose was cold. I slowly sat down on the bench Dad had made.

The pup was next, and he wasn't nearly as cautious. In about two minutes he was trying to untie my shoelaces. I let him.

The female moved around behind me and sniffed the back of my neck. It tickled, and I suddenly wanted to laugh and laugh, this was so wonderful. But I stayed quiet.

All this time the male alpha stood a little way off, watching like a dad watching his family. He never did come right up to me that day, but I had the feeling he approved.

I looked around to see if Ruthie was anywhere near. Once I thought I saw a shadow move back in the trees, but

I wasn't sure it was she. I wanted to talk to her, tell her it was surprising but okay, but I didn't think I ought to lead them to her den. And I knew they'd follow me.

The pup was trying to get my sneakers off now.

"Hey," I said, "enough is enough." I gave him a gentle push, and he bounded right back. The yearling moved in and gave him a shove, and the two began to wrestle.

All of a sudden all of them froze in place. I couldn't hear a thing. Was it Ruthie? I looked around but saw nothing there. Then with a speed and silence I could hardly believe, they were gone back into the woods—not a sign of a wolf.

Suddenly I heard what they had heard: Dad's pickup churning up the trail. Help!

I was almost to the front door when the pickup chugged in, in a cloud of dust.

"You're early," I said. "Mom's still in town."

"I'm in a hurry." He jumped out and left the door open. "We're going to do a special in Glacier Park. Some kind of big-shot conference on the environment." He rushed into the house and began throwing things into a backpack: socks, underwear, clean T-shirts, toothbrush, and razor.

"How long are you going to be gone?"

"I'm not sure. Two or three days, I guess. Tell your mother I'll call her tonight, maybe late."

I felt weak with relief. Saved by the environment! For a few days anyway. By the time he got back, the wolves would be settled in, and Mom would help me persuade him it was okay.

He zipped the backpack. "We'll be bivouacked at the McDonald."

He checked his wallet for cash and put a twenty on

the kitchen table. "Tell her she can cash a check if she runs out."

I never can get over men. He was giving her permission to cash a check! My mom has had her own checking account all our lives. She didn't need permission. She has her own money, saved from her job, and royalties on the book she illustrated, and money Nonny sends fairly often.

"I'll tell her she has your permission," I said.

He didn't even get it. "Take care of things," he said. He shoved his straw cowboy hat onto the back of his head. "When I'm away, I count on you to be the man of the house."

What do you do? Scream? Laugh? I said, "I'm the second woman in command here." But he didn't hear me. He was already out the door, scrambling into the pickup.

I saw him glance back. I looked. The female wolf was standing in the trees watching him, just barely in sight. He didn't react, so I guess he thought it was Ruthie. He waved, gave a cowboy yell, and took off. I sat down on the steps to pull myself together.

CHAPTER 17

I took out of my pocket the envelope the guy had given me. I'd almost forgotten it, but it was in my hip pocket, and it made a bulge when I sat down.

There was a certificate of ownership, something like the one Mom had left for A. Dolan. It said that Arthur Washington had given his four wolves, which he had raised from infancy, to the family of McDougall, resident on un-named dirt road, and then it gave the exact distance from Bigfork, like some kind of explorer's map. No compensation was involved, the paper said; the wolves were the property of the McDougall family, to have and to hold for all time, on condition only that they not be sold, given to a zoo, or otherwise disposed of without first notifying said Arthur Washington. It sounded like a will or something.

There were four certificates from a woman vet in

Whitefish, stating that the wolves had had rabies shots. I hadn't thought about getting one for Ruthie, but I decided I would. You could never tell when there might be a rabid skunk or something wandering around.

The next piece of paper said, "Names of wolves, subject to change at the will of the new owners. Alpha male: Marcus Aurelius; female: Diantha; Yearling: Geoffrey Bingham; Pup: Buster."

Well, subject to change, all right! Can you imagine tossing a bloody chunk of raw meat to Marcus Aurelius? Or playing who's got the shoestring with Geoffrey Bingham?

The last piece of paper had a yellow Post-It attached that said, "Start-up money, with best wishes and a thousand thanks, Arthur." The note was written in a hurried-looking scrawl. The paper the Post-It was attached to was a postal money order for five hundred dollars, made out to Lee McDougall. The "Lee" was scribbled in with a different pen. I couldn't believe it.

It would be good to have that money for wolf food. That would partly demolish Dad's arguments. Five hundred dollars would buy a fair amount of meat. At least I thought it would. I wasn't really sure what meat cost.

I sat on my bed and tried to calm down. I knew if Mom let us keep the wolves, I'd be responsible for them. My own pack of wolves. It was daunting.

A great idea hit me. My book about Ruthie, which kept getting stalled, would have a lot to go on now. I had a whole pack to write a book about, and I bet there'd be plenty of conflict.

CHAPTER 18

Mom came home alone, and again the wolves just melted into the trees when they heard the car coming.

"Where's Savannah?" I said.

"She's going to the play and staying overnight with Allie Johannson."

"Mom, you know, don't you, those kids Savannah hangs out with are about three or four years older than she is."

"I know that, but they're interested in the theater. They seem like nice enough kids, and I've met Allie's mother. They have a place on the lake."

"Savannah's growing up faster than I am."

"Well, there aren't any exact measurements about that, I guess." She looked at her watch. "Your father's late."

I told her where he'd gone. I was so nervous over telling her about the wolves, I'd forgotten about Dad. "He'll call you tonight."

"Oh, good. We won't have to fix a real dinner. Look through the cans and the frozen stuff and see what appeals to you. There's raspberry-chocolate-truffle ice cream for dessert."

"And Savannah's not here to gobble it all up." I looked into the frozen food compartment and found some creamed chipped beef. "How about this on toast?"

"Good."

From the woods, riveting me to the spot, came a long mournful howl.

"You didn't forget to feed Ruthie, did you?"

"Mom, I have something to tell you."

"Oh, dear. That's the most terrifying sentence I know."

"It's not really terrifying. But you'd better sit down."

The howl came again, with a second and a third joining in, and then a series of sharp barks.

Mom gave me a look and dashed out the back door. Believe me, I was right behind her.

The four wolves were huddled together near the place where I'd left the water buckets. They were telling me they were hungry.

"Good heavens!" Mom said. "I'm not hallucinating?"

"No, I was going to tell you. See, this guy called up. . . ." I tried to tell the story as briefly as I could.

Mom sighed. "And of course you couldn't say no."

"Would you?"

"How do we know they aren't stolen or something?"

I had to grin. "You mean like Ruthie?"

"I paid fifty dollars for Ruthie, and you know it. Oh, what is your father going to say! Think what it will cost!"

"He left five hundred dollars."

Her mouth fell open. "Are you serious?"

"I don't kid about five hundred dollars. It's a money order, made out to me."

"Five hundred dollars. Well, that will mollify your father to some extent. They're handsome creatures."

I began to relax. She was hooked. "I'll get them some meat."

I ran back, while Mom opened the gate and went inside to meet our new family members.

They were inspecting her from a cautious distance, except for Buster, when I came back with the meat. Buster was already tugging at her shoestrings. Shoestrings seemed to be his big turn-on.

But they forgot Mom and raced for the fence when they smelled the meat. I tossed the chunks over the fence. The others held back while the alpha ate, and then he moved aside for the female. In a few minutes all of them were happily chomping away.

Suddenly the yearling stopped eating and growled. He was looking over his shoulder.

"Look," Mom said.

Ruthie was peering timidly through the trees.

The yearling growled again.

"Oh, no, my hearty, none of that." Mom went right over to him and pushed him gently. I held my breath. She found a chunk of meat that no one had claimed and took it over to Ruthie.

Ruthie ate it, keeping an eye on the other wolves, who were now paying no attention to her.

Mom and I sat down on the warm pine needles and watched them eat.

"Is this their first meeting with Ruthie?"

"As far as I know."

"They won't take her in, you know, but I suppose they'll tolerate her."

"Poor Ruthie."

"How old is the young one?"

"Five months."

"I'd love to do a study of him as he grows up. I wonder if anyone at the university would be interested."

"Hey, that would be great! With drawings and all?"

"We'll think about it. Have you thought about Savannah's reaction to four more wolves?"

"Hysteria."

"Yes. Well, she seems to have pretty much forgotten about Ruthie. She'll just have to get used to these. Thank goodness she's all wrapped up in the theater. She's angling for a walk-on in their next show."

"If Savannah is angling, Savannah will get it."

We watched while the wolves finished eating and lolled around on the grass. Only the pup had enough energy left over to tease the other wolves.

"Look at Ruthie," Mom said.

Very slowly, Ruthie was moving toward them, practically crawling on her belly, her ears flattened against her lowered head.

"She looks like somebody applying for a job," Mom said.

I wished Ruthie would just hold up her head and walk right in and say, "Hi, gang, mind if I join you?" But that's not the way it works.

The wolves watched her indifferently. The pup of course was the one who finally went up to her. She sank even lower into the ground, if possible, while he sniffed her all over. His tail was lifted, but hers was spread flat on the ground. He backed up and stared hard at Ruthie, who lowered her eyes. Then he stood stiff-legged across her front legs. She didn't move. With a toss of his bossy puppy head, he trotted back to his family and lay down.

" 'That's that,' he's saying," Mom said. "No problem."

"I don't see why they can't be nicer to her."

"Because she's not one of them. Take a look at human beings, honey, if you want comparison. Let's go have that chipped beef. I'm starved."

So Mom was on my side, and that was important, but we had Dad and Savannah to deal with, and that was not going to be any cinch.

CHAPTER 19

When we got to the ice cream, Mom said, "Do we know who this man is and where he can be found if your father puts his foot down or if Savannah works up a state of psychosis, or both?"

"He can't be found. He was taking off right away. He said, 'If you ever come to Europe, let me know.' "

"Not exactly precise. Is he fleeing the FBI or anything?"

"He's fleeing his wife."

"Oh." She got us both some more ice cream.

"Mom, who exactly was Marcus Aurelius?"

"Marcus Aurelius, *The Meditations of*—Roman philosopher, second century, I think. The one quote I remember is: 'The intelligence of the universe is social. Accordingly, it has made the inferior things for the sake of the superior, and it has fitted the superior to one another.' It sounds like Hitler to me. Race superiority."

"Well, that's the name of the alpha wolf. The boss."

"Ah. What are the others' names?"

"The female is Diantha."

"Oh. Dianthus is a lovely flower."

"But is it a wolf?"

I had to go get the man's papers to find the name of the yearling. "Geoffrey Bingham."

She looked surprised. "Geoffrey Bingham was the name of a character in a TV series. I think there are books too. Suspense stuff. Once when I was still living with Nonny, I met the author. He was trying to peddle the series and getting nowhere. What was his name . . . Jefferson? Lincoln?"

"Washington," I said. "Arthur."

She was amazed. "How do you know that?"

"Those are his wolves."

She leaned back so far in her chair I thought she was going over backward. "Are you telling me . . . ?"

"That was Arthur Washington who came with the wolves." I showed her the papers.

She was flabbergasted. "You know something?" she said. "I mean something really weird? I was about nineteen when I met Arthur Washington, and I had a mad crush on him. Of course he didn't notice me at all. He was trying to get Nonny to invest in his show."

I was knocked over. "He's handsome. He looks like an old Garth Brooks."

"Old?" Mom made a face. "I guess he would be."

"Well, I mean he's an older man. But he's a knockout. If you'd married him . . ."

"Then you and Savannah wouldn't exist, but I'd probably have the wolves." She laughed. "No chance. He hardly knew I existed. I think he's had four or five wives."

"Well, he's trying to get rid of the one he has now. I'm grateful to her, 'cause I get the wolves."

"The wolves, yes." Mom poured herself a cup of coffee. "Back to reality. Your dad's not going to like it. The official cattle growers' association is antiwolf."

"Why does anybody have to know about them?"

"Are you serious? With your sister around?"

"You don't think anybody'd try to hurt the wolves, do you?"

"I think there are people who would love to shoot them dead. But they are an endangered species, and it's against the law to kill them."

"Are you going to tell Dad when he calls tonight?"

She thought about it. "Let's wait till he comes home. He's got enough on his mind at the moment."

"We'll need more meat right away."

"Tomorrow you and I will go into town and load up. Maybe we can have a picnic at the lake first. I'll call Savannah in the morning and see if she wants to join us."

She stirred her coffee thoughtfully. "If I can get a book out of young pup out there, it would be practical from your dad's viewpoint."

I was thinking of my own book, a picture book with Ruthie as the outcast who gradually persuades the others to be friends. I'm not sure she'll be able to do that in real life, but in my book maybe she could. My English teacher says you have to invent to get a story—not just report.

We went out to see the wolves after Dad's call. He had sounded happy. He loves meeting people.

The wolves were standing huddled together, as if trying to psych out where they were. I got the hose and refilled the water buckets.

"Your dad can make a watering trough for them," she said. "If we get him involved, he'll be happier about the whole thing."

I laughed. "You're a conniver."

"Yep." She went over to the wolves and talked to them. The pup and the yearling began to wrestle, showing off. Occasionally the female got into it. She seemed almost as playful as her pup. Her coat was silver-gray, the pup was white, and the yearling was dark brown with white hind legs. It was beginning to be easy to tell them apart even when they got all mixed up together. The alpha was the only one with blue eyes. The pup and the female had dark eyes, and the yearling's were golden. I had to think of names for them.

I left them and went to find Ruthie. She was not far off, hiding in the trees where she could watch them. I tried to talk to her, but she wasn't interested in me. I couldn't tell if she felt frightened of the new wolves or was just curious, but she sure wasn't going to rush in and try to make friends.

I think Mom was almost as reluctant to leave them as I was.

Before I went to sleep, I worked out names for them. I'd call the alpha male Thunder. The female would be Silver. The yearling—I couldn't think. The pup was white, so he could be Snow. How about a Greek hero's name for the yearling? Maybe Prometheus—the one who stole fire from the gods. Oh, my beautiful family!

CHAPTER 20

When Mom called Savannah, Mrs. Johannson said Allie and Savannah were already at the beach.

Mom was a little annoyed when she hung up. "I've got to have a talk with Savannah about letting me know where she is. I don't like her just running around wherever she pleases."

I smiled to myself. Keeping track of Savannah was not a job I'd want to take on.

When we got to the beach, there were about a dozen kids there, including Savannah, who went into a scene of big dramatic surprise at seeing us, as if we'd just popped in from Uranus.

Bryan, the boy who was lifeguard at the pool, was there too, but he looked different. At the pool when I talked to him, I always had to look up at him on that high lifeguard chair, and my impression of him was mostly long brown legs and a hand with a megaphone in it, and somewhere up toward the sky a brown face with dark eyes. Here he looked more all of a piece. He was wearing long white denims and a T-shirt with a University of Montana logo. He came over, and I introduced him to my mother.

"I'm going to look for shells," Mom said, and wandered off.

Bryan sat down beside me. "Where've you been?"

"Oh, around," I said. "Don't you work at the pool anymore?"

"No. I got a better job, caretaker for some rich people who are in Europe. I got a neat little apartment in a boathouse. Well, not exactly an apartment, but a bed and a chair and table and a shower and all. And I'm allowed to use their catamaran. Maybe you'll come for a ride sometime. Makes me feel like I'm back in Hawaii."

He had never said so much to me before. I was dying to tell him about the wolves, but Mom and I had agreed to keep it a secret as long as we could. So we talked about other things, mostly Hawaii and what it was like growing up on the Big Island. He was from Hilo. His mother was pure Hawaiian, and his dad was a *baole*, which means from the mainland. Both of them were music teachers.

When Mom came back she invited him to share our picnic lunch, but he had to go back to work. He was very polite, and Mom approved of him.

Savannah joined us for the food and said, "Isn't Bryan cute? He asked me to go to the movies, but I couldn't make it."

Crash. Smash. Sun falls into the sea, world turns black. Sisters should be against the law.

While I was reeling from that blow, she said in a low voice, "I'm not supposed to tell yet, but I'm *probably* going to get a walk-on in next week's show." She leaned back and waited for us to faint.

"How'd you wangle that?" Mom said.

She frowned. "I didn't *wangle* it, Mother. The stage manager happened to see me on TV, and I think it was he who recommended me."

I wiped the mayonnaise off my chin. "Does he happen to know you're Savannah Saxton's grandkid, and does he happen to be going to the coast in the fall and would love an introduction?"

"I haven't the faintest idea where he's going in the fall. I don't ask personal questions." She pointed to a group farther down the beach. "He's the tall one, standing up."

He was tall all right, and very skinny, the kind of guy who looks like a cadaver in swim trunks. He had on a powder blue cap with a huge visor and Serengeti shades.

"And anyway, Lee," she said, "why do you always have to dump on my career?"

"Excuse *me*," I said. "I didn't know you had a career."

Mom said, "I'm going for a quick swim. If you're going home with me, make it five minutes." She ran toward the lake.

"I think I'll just join my theater friends for a while." Savannah sauntered down the beach.

I watched her join them. It didn't seem to me that any of them were paying much attention to her except Mr. Serengeti shades. He seemed to be talking up a storm. But she moved away from him. Was he a Lolita-type guy or what? I'd better warn her. Not that she'd listen.

I took a fast swim. Mom and I rubbed each other's backs with the beach towel, put on our shorts and T-shirts, and left. Mom looked grim.

"What's the matter?"

"I'm just thinking," she said, "about having to go to town every night next week at eleven or midnight to pick up my daughter, the star. I'm not cut out to be a stage mother."

"Well, tell her she can't do it."

"Are you joking? She'd be on the phone to Mother in five minutes, and you know the rest. My mother starred in her first ballet recital when she was five, and she never looked back."

"Maybe Savannah will get bored with it. Or outgrow it."

"Not a chance. This is act one, scene one, curtain. Or lights, camera, action." We drove past the theater group, and Savannah waved gaily. "In my day actors didn't loll about on the beach. They *worked*."

"Maybe they're rehearsing. Reading lines to one another."

"They don't look it. Well, thank heaven you're into something I can relate to, like wolves." She was driving faster than she usually does, and somebody blew his horn when she cut in front of him. "But I want everybody to know right now"—she scowled in the rearview mirror at the man who had honked—"I am not going to be a stage mother."

"You're going to be a wolf mother?"

That made her laugh.

We filled the trunk and the backseat with packages of meat, and Mom bought two large pizzas, which were definitely not for the wolves.

Mom had bought a secondhand refrigerator that we kept beside the freezer, so each day's supply of meat would be thawed out. We were heaving the heavy packages into that and into the freezer when I looked up and saw Ruthie trying to get a drink from one of the buckets, and Snow pushing her away. She put her tail between her legs, lowered her head, and left.

I ran over and yelled at Snow. "Stop being a big bully! Ruthie was here before you were."

He gave me a look—I swear he looked amused—and then he trotted off to join his mother, as if that was what he had meant to do anyway. I tried to call Ruthie back, but she wouldn't come.

Mom stood watching them. "You say Arthur said they wouldn't hurt her?"

I laughed. "That's what Arthur said, Mom. And Arthur knows." I enjoyed teasing her a little. It was interesting to think about your mother as a teenager with a crush on some handsome older guy.

In the house she said, "That seemed like a nice boy who talked to you at the beach. Is he Hawaiian?"

"Half. He *is* nice." I told her how I knew him a little at the pool. "He asked me today if I'd like a ride in a catamaran. He can use the one where he caretakes."

She gave me a sideways look. "Why didn't you say that when Savannah was bragging about his asking her to go to the movies?"

I shrugged.

"Listen, take a word of advice from another Savannah victim: Don't be a satellite."

"What do you mean?"

"The world is full of people shouting, 'Make way! Make way for Savannahs!' Don't do it. Stay in your own orbit."

"I don't know if I know what you mean."

"You know perfectly well what I mean. Think about it." She curled up in the armchair to watch the news on CNN, and I went back outside to fool around with the wolves.

I did know what she meant. I wished I could give Ruthie the same message: Make way for nobody.

CHAPTER 21

I decided to walk all the way around our property to make sure the fence was tight. Snow and Prometheus came with me. Silver wanted to; she started after us, but then she looked back at Thunder, standing there like the lord of the planet, and went back.

"Silver," I said, "come on. Don't be a plaything of the dominant sex. Let Thunder do the dishes and sweep up. Come with us."

But who was I to disturb the cultural patterns of fifty thousand years? Beautiful Silver stayed where she was, and we slogged along without her.

Very soon I realized that Ruthie was tagging along behind us at a respectful distance, ready to melt away if anyone said boo.

Neither Snow nor Prometheus paid any attention to

her. I spoke to her, and she pricked her ears forward, but she kept a certain distance behind us. She was really looking a lot better. Her body had filled out, her coat was beginning to come in thick and pretty, and even though, I guessed, she would always be the outsider, she didn't look as beaten down as she had once.

I thought about A. Dolan. The papers said the man who shot him had confessed and pleaded self-defense. The bartender testified that Dolan was falling-down drunk and very hostile. No verdict had been given yet. They found Dolan's gun in the dumpster, where the accused said he had thrown it after he got it away from Dolan and shot him. Life in the Wild West.

There were a lot of pretty things to look at in the woods in midsummer. Wild roses, some kind of yellow flower that I didn't recognize, sweet-smelling ferns, blue lupine, and that great canopy of trees over us with sunlight slanting through. I didn't think anymore about missing Missoula, it was so nice here. In Missoula I couldn't have had my wolves. I missed Holly though, and some of the other kids. I wondered what high school would be like up here. A lot smaller than Missoula's three schools. Holly would be at Hellgate. In Georgia people used to laugh when Mom said two of our schools were named Hellgate and Rattlesnake.

When we were at about the halfway point, we stopped. It had been hot and airless in the woods, but from this point you could look east toward open meadows and pastureland. Part of that, if I had my directions right, was the sheep ranch owned by a man named Sawyer. His wife had left, they said, and he lived there alone. He was one of those who wanted to keep wolves out of Montana. I hoped he had it straight in his head that our wolves were shut in and no danger to his sheep.

I shaded my eyes with my hand. I could see sheep grazing out there, looking like humpy gray dots. A boy named Donny worked for him. Donny was the one who shoved my head under in the pool, back when we first came. I had held him under till Bryan yelled at me to let him up before I drowned him. Ever since, Donny gave me a dirty look when I saw him downtown. I don't think Donny is very bright, and he is certainly mean.

Snow tugged at my shirt, and I said, "Okay, I'm coming"; but just as I turned away, I saw a glint in the distance, like a flashlight going on in the dark, only it was broad daylight. I squinted in that direction.

There was a man standing quite a distance away from us, leaning against a tree. He was tall and he had on a straw cowboy hat like my dad's. I was pretty sure it was Mr. Sawyer, because he had passed me once or twice (without speaking or even glancing at me) out in the forest where the road forks one way to our place and the other way to his ranch.

I started to wave, just to be neighborly, but then I saw what had caused the glint of light. He was looking at us through binoculars.

It gives you a weird feeling to know that somebody is staring at you through binoculars. He seemed to have the binoculars on a strap around his neck, because as far as I could tell they didn't fall to the ground when he dropped his hands.

I had to strain my eyes to see what he was doing, but

I could tell he moved a little and picked up something that leaned against the tree. The air was very still. I could hear insects humming, and a crow was flapping his way across the meadow, just about over our heads.

I saw that glint of light on metal again, and before I had time to react to it, the crow over our heads dropped like a stone just on the other side of the fence, and at the same time a gun roared.

At once, there was not a wolf in sight. And I ran as fast as I could all the way home, tripping over roots and deadfall and rocks, but never slowing down.

CHAPTER 22

The minute I finished telling Mom what had happened she piled me into the car and drove to the police station. Our old friend Officer McLaren was there.

He listened carefully to my story.

"Hobie Sawyer," he said. "I'm not surprised. The bank's threatened to take over his place if he doesn't ante up the mortgage payments, and I also heard some coyotes got three of his lambs last week."

"That's nothing to do with us," my mother said. "He shot at my child on our own property."

"But he hit the crow, and the bird, you say, was on his side of the fence when it fell."

I nodded.

"I know how you feel, Mrs. McDougall," he said, "but I don't see how's I can charge him with anything. I can warn him, and I will. Firing off a gun that close to somebody is willful negligence."

"It was a threat," I said.

"I know that, but you can't arrest a man for what's in his mind. It's all this blasted hullabaloo about wolves, about letting 'em into the parks and into the state, keepin' 'em on the endangered list so's they can't be shot. Everybody's riled up about it, petitioning and protesting and hollering their heads off, both sides."

"Whose side are you on?" I said.

"I'm not supposed to be on any side. To tell you the truth, I wouldn't know how to answer that anyway. This land sure enough belonged to the wolves and the deer and the bears and all the rest for a long time before we got here. On the other hand, we're here, ranches and towns and developments everywhere, and I don't know whether wolves should live alongside of us or not. Nobody's told them that deer they can have for supper, but lambs and calves they can't."

"Isn't there a fund that repays a rancher if he loses stock to a wolf?" Mom said.

"There is. A good chunk of money. But the rancher has to prove it was a wolf. Sometimes that's hard to do. Could be coyotes or just a pack of dogs." He shook his head. "It's a problem."

"Well, it's not our problem," Mom said, "except that now we've been shot at twice."

"If it's any consolation, I doubt either shot was meant to hit you. Old Dolan was just mad, and Sawyer's making a statement, as they say."

Mom got a grim look on her face. "Well, I think I will

drive out to Mr. Sawyer's place and make a statement myself."

Officer McLaren looked alarmed. "Ma'am, please don't do that. Hobie Sawyer is not in a very good frame of mind these days. He's desperate, in fact. He's right on the edge of losing everything he owns. He would not take kindly to interference."

"Interference!" Mom stood up.

He held out both hands, palms up. "I know, I know, but let me handle it, please. We don't want more trouble."

Mom scowled at him. "All right, but if anything happens to any of my family, or to any of our wolves for that matter, I'll throw the book at him."

"I know you will." Officer McLaren's expression was a mix of respect and amusement. I mean, my mother can be impressive. He held out his hand to her. "I promise you, I'll put the fear of God in him."

As I have noticed before, Officer McLaren is a very large man, solid muscle.

"All right," Mom said. "Thank you." She shook his huge hand.

In the car she was still muttering. "Guns," she said. "I'd like to get my hands on the man who invented gunpowder. And you can jolly well bet it was a man, not a woman."

"If it wasn't guns, it'd be broadswords," I said.

We drove by the theater. A bunch of people—actors, I guessed—were sitting around on the grass, some of them with scripts in their hands. And yes, there was my sister right in the middle of them. She didn't even see us.

Suddenly I got so mad, I wanted to get out and clobber her.

"Where does she get off, sitting around like she's a twenty-year-old TV star?"

Mom looked at me in surprise, then put her hand on mine. "You're shaking," she said. "Let's go home and have a cup of tea."

"I hate tea."

We drove home in silence.

"That was a scary experience," she said as we drove up to the cabin. "Getting shot at, even if he was only trying to frighten you. Come on in and I'll fix you a hot fudge sundae." She smiled at me.

"No, thanks." I knew she was being nice and I wasn't, but I didn't feel nice. And I wanted to make sure all the wolves were okay. All this talk about whether wolves belonged or not made me uneasy.

As soon as I went inside the gate, they came out to meet me. So they were safe this time, the four. They always hope I'm going to forget I fed them and do it again. I played with them a minute, then went looking for Ruthie. Snow started to follow, but I shooed him back. I knew they'd probably found out right away where her little den was, but in case they hadn't, I wasn't going to tell them. She wasn't in her den. I could see she was still using it though. There was a fresh bone inside the entrance, no meat left on it. I called her, but no Ruthie. I began to really worry. What if that man had fired his gun twice, so quickly that I only heard the one shot, and suppose one of the bullets had hit Ruthie?

I was shaking so hard that I had to hang on to a tree for a minute. It wasn't possible. I'd have heard two shots, even close together. Wouldn't I? In my mind I kept seeing that poor old crow just flying along, like the way you'd take a walk to enjoy the day, and suddenly blam! he or she was lying on the ground all bloody and busted up. I hoped he or she had died right off.

"Ruthie?" I began to walk through the woods. I didn't want to go anywhere near the Sawyer place, but if I didn't find her before I got to it, I'd have to. If she was just frightened, she wouldn't be there, that was for sure.

My heart was beating so fast, it made me feel choked. I wished I had a glass of water. The little stream was all dried up. Something touched the back of my knee, and I nearly fainted. Then I began to laugh, and then I was crying. It was Ruthie's cold nose. And it was the first time she'd ever touched me of her own accord.

I sat down hard on the ground and put my arms around her. And she let me hold her like that for several minutes.

"Did that moron scare you with his gun?" I scratched behind her ears. She seemed to like that. "He scared me, I can tell you. I thought we were all goners." I told her how we'd gone to the police, and how Mom got mad and told off Officer McLaren.

I told Ruthie about seeing my sister with the theater bunch and how mad it made me. "I don't know why. She's got a right to do what she wants to, I guess. I was just so tensed up and worried, and there she was, not a care in the world." I brushed Ruthie's coat with my fingers. It was getting nice and thick. "Well, she's not even twelve years old yet. I guess I should make allowances."

Ruthie chewed on my sleeve. I felt real good, because this was the first time she'd gotten close to me the way the other wolves did. She must have been starting to feel at home.

"And don't let those big-shot wolves push you around. You were the first, remember that. You're numero uno."

Lone wolf. I thought of that expression when I was walking back to the cabin. Dad had called me that once. Maybe that's why Ruthie and I understood each other.

When I got within sight of the cabin, I saw Dad's pickup parked in front. I braced myself for trouble.

CHAPTER 23

He was sitting in the kitchen with his feet up on another chair and a glass of iced tea in his hand. He has one of those faces you can't read if he doesn't want you to. The old cowboy poker face. I glanced at Mom. She didn't look upset, but she didn't give me any clue.

"Well, hey," he said. "How ya doin'?"

"All right. You have a good trip?"

"Wasn't exactly a trip. But yeah, it was real interesting." He studied my face. It made me nervous. Had Mom told him about the wolves or not? They hadn't been in the clearing when I came through—spooked by the sound of the pickup probably. They liked to check out the score before they showed up.

I waited.

He brought his boots down on the floor with a bang.

My father would like to be about six inches taller than he is, so he makes up for it in other ways, like being noisy.

"I go away for a couple days, and look what happens," he said.

"What?" I said feebly.

"What? My youngest kid becomes a theater star. My oldest kid takes on a pack of wolves. My favorite writer, Arthur Washington, shows up at my place and I'm not here to meet him. Left five hundred bucks. My oldest kid gets herself shot at by the neighbor, and my wife spends the morning with the fuzz."

"Is Arthur Washington really your favorite author?"

"One of 'em. He does a fine suspense story, and that TV series was pretty good too."

"Mom knows him."

"I just found that out. Guess it never came up before." He gave Mom a funny look.

I wondered if she'd told him she'd had a crush on Mr. Washington.

"Well, when does Vannie get home? I suppose she comes and goes in a limo now."

It was easy to see which of the things that had happened pleased him. "Do you want to see the wolves?"

He shrugged. "I've seen wolves. I hope they're better-looking than that mangy critter you brought home last time." Suddenly he grinned, and it changed his whole face. It was the only way you could ever tell he'd been kidding.

"Wait till you see Ruthie now. She looks good."

"And of course the new pack are celebrity wolves."

Mom and I exchanged glances. I read her look to mean it was going to be okay; he wasn't going to say get rid of them. I suppose this was because they had belonged to his favorite writer. I could hear him bragging to his friends: "You know that author Arthur Washington, big shot up there with Robert Parker and Stephen King. Had a TV series a while back. Well, he gave us this pack of pet wolves he'd raised . . ." And so on.

I went into my room and flopped on my bed. It had been a day.

CHAPTER 24

It was three days before Savannah discovered that we had a pack of wolves. She'd gotten the part in the new play, a little more than a walk-on, actually; she had two lines. Also she was understudy to two small parts. So she was over at the theater all afternoon every day, and often in the evenings with poor Mom having to sit through rehearsals to bring her home. Other people offered to give her a ride home, but Mom said no way.

And Savannah slept till noon every day, just like actors do, you know. So she didn't know about the wolves until the night they sang.

We hadn't heard them do that howling in chorus that wolves do, so when it started about two o'clock one morning, I didn't even think of Savannah.

Mom and I went into the kitchen to hear it better. I can't explain how beautiful it is, the way they harmonize, one voice coming in, and then another, till they're all singing together in different keys. They sang in chords, sometimes all but one dropping out, then coming back on a different note. It was like minor chords, but not dissonant, if that's what I mean.

One of them hit a high note, then lower down, and one by one the other voices fell away. The silence was like another world.

The whole thing lasted only about three minutes. Mom and I looked at each other, speechless. What can you say when something is that beautiful?

Dad's sleepy voice called out from their bedroom, "Hey! Nice concert."

Then Savannah staggered into the kitchen, still half-asleep, more confused than scared. "Did I dream that, or what?"

"Go back to bed, honey," Mom said. "I'll explain in the morning."

"I dreamed I heard these weird voices. . . ."

Mom steered her gently back to bed.

By the time she woke up at noon the next day, I think she thought it *had* been a dream. She was running late, so Mom didn't try to tell her. But on the way to the car she suddenly saw them, gathered in a group on the other side of the fence. She screamed.

"Get into the car," Mom said, "or you'll be late for rehearsal."

Well, you know what they say: The show must go on.

The next day before she left, she stood looking at them for a few minutes. Snow and Prometheus were batting each other around, and Silver whapped at them with one paw, lazily. Savannah didn't say a word.

Mom must have explained it all to her on their way into town. Savannah never mentioned the wolves to me until one night later in the summer. I suppose the theater was so much on her mind, she didn't have time to be scared of wolves.

When she was at home, she dragged me into her room to cue her on her lines and on the understudy parts. I got so sick of those lines, few as they were, I was ready to scream. Finally I got an idea: Without telling her, I taped the whole thing. Then afterward I erased her lines and just left the cues. All she had to do was use the tape for her cues. She didn't think it was such a brilliant idea, but she accepted it.

It wasn't until the night we went to the play that I got any notion of what those lines were all about. They were gibberish to me.

Opening night was hysteria night. Even Mom was in a state. I was mainly concerned with having to dress up. I hate dressing up.

Mom bought me a flared blue skirt that I rather liked, though, and with that and a white blouse with tiny buttons I got to wear my favorite thing in all the world, a pale blue cashmere cardigan that Nonny had sent me for Christmas.

We had aisle seats in the third row. The play was a new one, by somebody from the university. Something I've learned, I guess from Nonny, is it's no use asking an actor if a play is good, all they know is if their part is good. Savannah loved her part.

Savannah had told us she didn't come on till halfway through the first act. I found myself listening for the cue: A character named Prudence (Prudence?) was supposed to say, "I don't care what you say, I'm taking Gerald to the poetry reading tonight." I could have read that line backward in my sleep.

Mom was sitting quiet as a statue beside me, all tensed up. Dad was fidgeting.

Suddenly I heard the line. Prudence was halfway through before it hit me. I nearly jumped out of my seat. Mom grabbed my arm.

Then there was my sister, bounding onto the stage (she was supposed to be a bounding type), saying, "Where is Gerald?"

She looked so beautiful, it made my head ache. She was radiant. I heard somebody behind me gasp. For a second I thought they were going to applaud, and I was really afraid Dad would.

Her voice was just right, youthful and enthusiastic but not too girlish, not thin the way lots of kids' voices are. Of course Nonny had been bombarding her with letters and phone calls of advice.

When the audience laughed at her line, which they were supposed to do, I saw her raise her head and start to smile at them, and then remember not to. Nonny had told her over and over, "Remember there is a fourth wall in that room, the wall between you and the audience. You in your character are not aware of any audience. Only an amateur ever acknowledges the existence of an audience except during curtain calls." Savannah is so used to charming people, it was hard for her not to beam at these. But she remembered.

For an unpleasant minute I hoped she'd forget; not blow it, but just make some small mistake, something *human*. A kid sister who goes through life like a goddess can get hard to live with, you know?

But then I nobly thrust such thoughts from my mind, and I really was proud of her. She moved well, she spoke well, her face did the right things, she acted as if she had been "born in a trunk" like the Judy Garland song. Mom must have known in her bones when she named her Savannah.

I sneaked a quick look at Mom. She was beaming; she was proud. She wasn't thinking, Oh, not another Savannah to put up with! She might think that tomorrow, but not now.

The least I could do was feel the same.

Savannah's second line came almost at the end of the act.

Cue from character named Jason: "You don't have enough soul for Gerald, Polly."

Polly (Savannah), with a slight distortion of Shakespeare: "There are more things in heaven and earth, dear Jason, than you have ever dreamed on."

It brought down the house, and she made her exit to loud applause. She had had a lot of trouble with that line, but tonight she said it perfectly: just the slightest touch of sexiness with an overlay of girlish innocence. I wondered if anybody in the house except her family would believe that she wouldn't be twelve for two weeks.

Since the women she had understudied had all remained revoltingly healthy, she had no more to do. I could imagine her backstage, graciously accepting congratulations from the crew, going into the makeshift dressing room she shared with two other women, inhaling the flowers from us and from Nonny. (Nonny's had come with a card saying, "Break a leg, my darling.") And there were more flowers from friends of hers I didn't even know.

I didn't pay much attention to the rest of the play. I was thinking about Savannah. Would she really go on to stardom, or would she fizzle out, a cute child actress? She wasn't "cute," though. She already had grown-up poise. And Nonny would see to it that she did the right things.

And what about me? Would I ever sell a book? Do some decent, acceptable drawings? I didn't want to illustrate nonfiction books on flora and fauna the way Mom did. I wanted to do stories for kids. I wasn't getting very far with the Ruthie book. During the rest of the play, while people around me laughed and clapped, I was completely lost in the story of Ruthie, trying to figure out how to get it right.

My father nudged me. "Clap!"

The cast was taking a curtain call, my sister at the end of the line almost standing on tiptoe to be seen. Then, while Dad went out to the lobby to make sure the photographer from the station was there, people were congratulating Mom on her child, and Mom was saying, "And this is my writer and artist daughter."

Nobody looked impressed. I wished Mom would pretend she didn't know me.

We had to wait forever while the crowd slowly cleared

out and the photographer took a million pictures. And then we had to go to an opening night party at somebody's lake house. It was pretty, I have to admit. The house was set back from the lake, and there were Japanese lanterns hung from the trees. Little booths here and there had food and drinks, and waiters moved around serving people. One of them looked familiar, and I finally realized it was that Donny, the kid I shoved down in the pool.

I didn't know anybody, and after I got some food, I tried to get away down to the lake. But a tall, skinny guy stopped me and said, "Aren't you Savannah's sister?"

I admitted it. He looked like somebody I'd seen, maybe an actor, but then I realized it was the stage manager. "Where are your Serengeti shades?" I said. He was wearing normal glasses.

He grinned. "It's dark out. Look, my name is Doug Waterson, and I'd like to talk to you. I'm pushed for time till the season's over, but could I come take some pictures of your wolves? Ever since I heard Savannah talking about that almost-dead little wolf she saved—"

I interrupted him. "Why do you say 'wolves,' plural?"

"Oh, everybody's heard about the new pack. Some idiots were screaming about it at the council meeting. . . . Don't you read the paper?"

He annoyed me. And I didn't like the idea that everybody knew we had the new wolves. "Sorry, no pictures, no visitors."

He opened his mouth to say more, but some people swooped down on him, gushing about the play. I walked down the slope to the lake. Nobody was around, although the dock had Japanese lanterns strung around it. I sat down on one of the pilings.

What was it with that Doug guy anyway? Did he think he could sell pictures of my wolves? Or was he after my sister? I thought I'd better warn Savannah to keep her distance.

The moonlight and the colored lights were reflected in the water. The lake was very still. Somewhere in the woods an owl hooted.

"I'm with you, Owl," I said. "I don't belong here either."

A voice from the water near me said, "Aloha, Lee."

I nearly jumped off the dock. It was Bryan, sitting in the middle of a canoe, paddling slowly with a double-bladed paddle. He drifted closer in.

"Enjoying the party?"

"It's better from here."

"Yes, it is."

My mother was looking for me. I could see her. "I guess I have to go," I said.

"Don't forget, someday we'll have that ride in the catamaran before summer is over." Silently, with hardly a ripple in the water, he was gone. I was glad he had come along. He seemed like part of the lake somehow.

I joined Mom, and finally we were on our way home. For once Savannah was so overcome, she didn't have much to say. But you could almost feel the rays of happiness coming out of her. Even Dad was quiet.

Before we got to our road, Savannah slumped against me and fell sound asleep with her head on my shoulder.

I looked down at her face. She has these delicately

arched dark eyebrows, in spite of being a blond, and unbelievably long, curling eyelashes. She had a smudge of mascara on her cheek, and all the hugging and congratulating had mussed up her hair.

Gently, so as not to wake her, I laid my cheek against the top of her head.

CHAPTER 25

Savannah slept almost all the next day. I spent most of the morning sketching the wolves and taking pictures of them with my new camera. The pictures would help, because naturally just when a wolf got into a position I wanted him to hold, he thought of something better to do. Mostly they wanted to grab my sketching pencil and run with it.

When I came in for lunch, Mom was on the phone with Nonny, telling her how well Savannah had done. I was surprised that Nonny was up so early—ten o'clock California time. She was one of those sleepers-till-noon when she wasn't working on a picture.

"You'd have been proud, Mother," Mom was saying. "She did everything right, and she looked beautiful. I found myself crying, and you know what a tough old bird I am."

I had to smile at the thought of my tenderhearted mom thinking she was tough.

Then her voice changed. "What doctor?" She listened intently. "Oh, for your contact lenses. You scared me for a second. . . . Yes, darling, I know, never a sick day since you had the mumps, aged six. Here's Lee to say hello."

"Hi, Nonny," I said. It was always so good to hear that beautiful voice. "Your granddaughter did herself proud."

"Oh, Lee, I'd have died to be there. And I would have been if it hadn't been for these stupid doctor appointments."

Plural? Did you need more than one appointment to get your contacts changed? Probably you did. I'd never had to wear glasses or contacts yet.

"Maybe she'll get a small part in the last show," I said. "I think she's got her hook out."

"Hook?" Nonny sounded vague for a second. "Oh, fishing." She laughed. "How is your drawing going?"

"Well, I'm having fun. I'm working on the wolves." Had Mom told her about the wolves? I glanced at her, and she nodded. Sometimes she just reads my mind.

"They must be beautiful. Darling Lee, I'll tell you a secret. I haven't even told your mother. Remember how you and I used to have our secrets?"

"You bet!" I'd always loved that.

"If Savannah gets a part in the last play—let's see, what dates would that be? Where's my calendar. . . . Lee, darling, if Savannah gets the part, call me, *secretly!* I may just be able to come."

"Nonny! You mean it?"

"Barring any nasty interferences. But not a word, remember. I must go, before I own AT&T. I love you, darling."

"Love you too, Nonny."

Mom smiled when I hung up. "From the glow on your face, I know you and your grandmother have one of your secrets. I won't even try to guess."

"Right. It's a doozy." I had to go out to tell the wolves that possibly, just possibly, they might get to know Nonny.

Savannah got up just in time to take a long shower, eat a little, and spend hours making up.

I stopped in her doorway and watched her. "Don't they have a makeup person?"

"Of course. But I like to do my own foundation." She did not sound friendly. What had I done now?

"You were on the noon news."

That got her attention. "Why didn't somebody wake me?"

"Well, it was just a shot of the cast and an interview with the director. Dan did it. You looked good."

She gave me a look. "Well, thanks for something. I know you thought I was a flop."

I was shocked. "What a stupid thing to say. You were great."

"You never said so last night."

"Was I supposed to push through your crowd of well-wishers at that party and tell you I approved? And that reminds me, this Doug guy, what's his problem?"

"Oh, I can't get him off my back. He thought I was the one with the wolves. Kept asking me how old they were, what sex, what this, what that."

"And you didn't know."

"Of course I didn't know, or care. I finally told him I'd turned them over to you."

"Turned them over to me. Well, thanks a bunch."

"You could have told me on the way home you liked my performance."

"You happened to be asleep on my shoulder." So much for those loving sisterly thoughts I'd had last night.

Mom called me into the kitchen, and Savannah went into her room.

"Don't let Van upset you," Mom said. "It's day-after-opening-night nerves. I had to live with it for years."

"I didn't think she cared about my opinion anyway."

Mom put her arm around me. "She cares about yours more than anybody's. You just have to learn the technique of living happily with an actor, bless them. Do you want to see the show tonight?"

"No, not really."

"Dad is going, but I think I'll stay home. I had some encouraging noises from a biology man I know at the university about doing a study of young Snow."

"Hey, that's great."

"He's sending me some material from the university's library so I can see what's been done along those lines."

"That's terrific." I went outside. Ruthie was peeking from a clump of huckleberry bushes, and the other wolves were lying down digesting their dinner. I told Snow he might become famous.

Then I sat down with Ruthie and told her about Savannah and the play and the man who wanted to take her picture. "But don't worry, none of that." I told her about sitting on the dock. "You and I are loners. But we have to be real loners, not eat our hearts out over what other people say or don't say. You and me, we'll tell each other our troubles. And don't forget, you're the heroine of my book. Lupe, Queen of the Forest."

She looked at me with those eyes that seem to understand every word. I stretched out beside her and put my arm around her. And she let me. That was the nicest part.

CHAPTER 26

Mom and Dad took turns taking Savannah to the play. I went once more with Mom, but I wouldn't go if it meant leaving the wolves alone. I had started reading the paper, and that guy was right, there was a big argument going on about our wolves and wolves in general. It's hard to understand why they get so wrought up over wolves. Nobody screams about coyotes or mountain lions. Maybe because wolves are protected by the Endangered Species Act, and no one is supposed to kill them.

The second time I saw the play, I thought the energy was down a little, but that was understandable. We went backstage, and I mashed myself against the back flap to keep out of the way. There's always such a hubbub backstage.

I hoped I wouldn't run into the stage manager, but of course there he was, wearing steel-rimmed granny glasses like some sixties type, scurrying around doing what stage managers do, which is everything. He almost crashed into me with a chair in his arms.

"Sorry," he said, shoving by me. And then he got this wild look of recognition and said, "Oh, it's you! I haven't forgotten. After all this summer madness passes, we have to talk. Important! Oops!" He had bumped into the leading man this time. And then he was gone somewhere into the darkness where they stored the sets. A real nut case, that guy.

Savannah had changed, and Mom was firmly prying her loose from her friends.

Finally we were in the car heading home, Savannah breathing heavily and unable to sit still. "Only one more night," she said. "I can't bear to have it close. There's going to be a party. You're invited, Lee."

"That's nice," I said, "but I don't think so. I mean those aren't people I know. I feel like a loose BB gun wandering around that crowd." That Sawyer guy was on my mind.

Savannah was being nice. "That's all right, Lee. You're not the party type anyway."

I started to ask what type I was, but I decided I'd better not. She might tell me.

"You're invited too, Mom."

"Let Dad take you. He's the party type," Mom said.

Finally, after a few false starts, Savannah said, "Look, I'm not supposed to breathe a word of this till the play is over and some of the cast, I won't say who, have left, but"— she took a deep breath—"I am going to have a part in the last play of the season! A real part with lines."

There was just the slightest pause before Mom said, a little too heartily, "That's wonderful, honey. Congratulations."

"Great, Savannah," I said. "Is that next week?"

"No, no. We have to rehearse. Next week a university cast is doing *Fiddler on the Roof*. Ours will close the season. Oh, wait till I tell Nonny!"

"She'll be thrilled," Mom said.

I knew she was thinking, Stage mother in spite of myself.

She turned into the forest road, and we braced ourselves for the bumps. It was eerie driving into the forest in the pitch dark. Mom had to drive slowly so she wouldn't get off the trail.

"I just found out something tonight," Savannah said. "When we were talking about my new part, Jerry told me it was Doug Waterson—you know, the stage manager?— who recommended me for this show. After he saw me on TV. I thought I'd heard that before, but I wasn't sure it was true."

"Do directors let stage managers do casting?" Mom said.

"Well, that's another thing I didn't know: He's quite rich. He owns part of the company. I wish I'd known that."

"Why?" I said.

"Well, I'd have been nicer to him."

"Because he's rich?" Mom sounded shocked.

"Well, not that exactly, but he's probably a more interesting person than I realized."

"Because he's rich?" I said it this time. "Savannah, that's gross."

"Oh, forget it," she said.

I got ready to open the car door and get out to let us through the gate.

Mom stopped the car so suddenly that I bumped into the dash.

"Hurry up," Savannah said from the backseat. "I'm beat. Open the gate, Lee."

"Take a look." My own voice sounded weird in my ears.

Savannah leaned forward. She gasped and said, "Oh, no!"

Our new gate had been smashed in. Pieces of it lay all over the road and in the bushes.

For a minute none of us said anything. Then I got out. Our two signs were hanging crookedly on the fence posts. The posts themselves were knocked off-balance, leaning crazily like some kind of scene after a bombing.

The signs had been painted over in dripping black paint. One of them said GET OUT. The other one said KILL ALL WOLVES. For one moment I couldn't move. Then I jumped back into the car.

"Get home quick! The wolves . . ."

I really expected to find five dead wolves. I jumped out of the car before it stopped and ran into the enclosure, calling them.

They came out slowly, as they always do, but they came. At the tag end, Ruthie poked her nose out from a clump of trees. My legs gave out, and I sat down hard on the ground.

I heard Savannah say in a scared voice, "Mom, she has to send those wolves away. We're all in danger."

CHAPTER 27

I heard Dad's pickup come as far as the broken gate and stop. From where I sat, with Ruthie's head in my lap and the other wolves clustered around me, I heard his angry voice, then Mom's quiet one. It didn't seem any time at all before a patrol car was there, and there was a lot of talk, Dad's voice the loudest. I didn't move.

The two patrolmen came down to the fence and looked in at us. Maybe because I was with them, and the officers didn't come inside, the wolves stayed where they were.

"Are they all right?" One of the officers flashed his light toward us, and Ruthie pulled away from me out of sight.

"Don't do that," I said. "Yes, they're all right."

"How many do you have?"

"Five."

The other officer gave a little whistle. "They seem to like you."

"Of course. They're my wolves." I wished they'd go away. Thunder was beginning to pace.

The first officer touched the top wire of the fence lightly and jumped. "Electrified. If I was you, I'd get an alarm system. Some people are nuts." His voice was kind.

"I know," I said. "We will."

They went away. After a while I said good-night to the wolves and went into the house. Mom and Dad and Savannah were sitting in the little living room, looking grim. Savannah stopped whatever she was saying when I came in.

"If you're talking about how I should get rid of the wolves," I said, "forget it." I went into my room and went to bed.

But I couldn't get to sleep. I had to think about it: Was I really putting my family at risk? The wolves wouldn't be any safer anywhere else. At least they could disappear into the woods if anyone came, and it wouldn't be easy to find them. Wolves are good hiders.

It was probably cruel to make Savannah live in fear, but we weren't going to be shot; she was just dramatizing again. The wolves were what people wanted to get rid of, not us. Killing a wolf is one thing, in the eyes of the law, but killing people is something else. Then I thought how easily A. Dolan got killed. Over nothing.

I didn't think I'd sleep at all that night, but I did. I woke early, but Dad was gone already, earlier than usual. I went out and fed the wolves and talked to them awhile.

When I came in, Mom was in her bathrobe, fixing breakfast. She looked as if she hadn't slept much. She put some pancakes on the table and got the bottle of maple syrup.

"What do you think?" I said finally. Somebody had to say something.

"I just don't know. Your father is on your side. He says nobody is going to scare him into giving up his own animals on his own land. But I know he's worried. And I'm trying to figure out if Savannah is as terrified as she seems."

"Probably. But a lot of places she'll live in in her life will be terrifying. Southern California isn't exactly Safe City. We left Alaska because it made her cough. In Germany she got it into her head that she was going to be gang-raped by drunken soldiers. Savannah sees life in TV scenes."

Mom smiled, sort of sadly. "She wants to live with Nonny. Maybe she should. I don't know. Are you happy here, Lee?"

"I have never been so happy anywhere in my life."

"Does what happened last night scare you?"

"Sure. But it makes me mad more than it scares me. We all know it was probably that weirdo next door."

She turned on the little TV set on the shelf just as the morning news came on. That was one of Dad's programs.

He usually looked pleasant and friendly, but this morning he looked grim. He gave some news about some new forest fires near the Idaho border, and a university budget problem that the legislature was trying to solve in its special session. Then he said: "A man and a juvenile were arrested in Bigfork early this morning after the police found their fingerprints on some defaced signs and a smashed gate in Barrett Woods. Apparently they used a pickup with a snow-blade attached to the front to do the damage. The man's name is Hobart Sawyer, a sheep rancher. The juvenile's name is being withheld. Sawyer will be arraigned at the county courthouse this morning. The juvenile will be charged in juvenile court. They will be charged with malicious mischief, damage to private property, and trespassing. Now for the weather . . ."

Mom turned it off. "And they'll be bailed out by tomorrow. If not sooner."

"You think so?" I'd begun counting on their being in jail, safely out of the way, for a little while at least.

"Sure they will. The sheep owners' association or the cattlemen's, or 'interested friends.' Look at all the fuss there was a while ago over those wolves in Nine Mile."

"They were wild."

"Nevertheless. It's a hot subject."

"Are you saying I shouldn't keep the wolves?"

"I'm not saying that at all." She sat down and pushed her hair off her forehead. "I don't know what I'm saying, but just be careful when you're walking around in the woods."

"I'll carry my Girl Scout knife at all times, the one with the bottle opener and the nail file." I was trying to lighten her up, and she did smile.

The phone rang, and of course it was for Savannah. She woke up cross; but as soon as she got on the phone, she was so happy and excited, the cabin almost quivered.

"Right away!" she was saying. "Twenty minutes max." She made some more joyous noises and hung up. "Guess what!"

"You got the part," I said.

"I did, I did! I have to leave right away for a book rehearsal."

I had learned in my career as a grandchild and sister of the theater that a book rehearsal is when the cast sits around a table and read their parts for the first time, straight through.

"I'll drive you in," Mom said. "You'd better come too, Lee. We'll do some shopping, and I'm due for one more interview at the college for that part-time job."

"No, thanks, I'll stay here." I knew she didn't want to leave me alone, but I wasn't going to leave the wolves alone either. "I need to do some practicing on the computer." Also I wanted to call Nonny and tell her Savannah had the part. I had promised.

They were gone in a very short time, Mom looking anxious about leaving me. I patted her shoulder. "Lightning never strikes twice."

"Did anyone ever prove that?" She smiled though. "What can I bring you?"

"Sawyer's head on a platter. But next to that, some of those frozen Snickers bars and some computer paper."

And then they were gone. Anxiety is contagious. I looked up every time I heard an unusual or even a usual sound, like the woodpecker hammering away at the dead tree behind the shed.

I got myself another glass of milk and sat down to think. A lot of people were against getting wolves back into Montana, but a lot of people were for it. If there was an organization that was for it, we ought to talk to them.

I vaguely remembered that the first time we talked to

the cop in town, he said something about Sawyer being close to losing his property to the bank. If he was gone, we'd all feel a lot safer. Most ranchers might object to the wolves, but I didn't believe they'd get violent.

In the phone book I found the listing of banks in the Yellow Pages. I called five of them before I found the one that held the mortgage on Sawyer's place. This guy was the first one who asked who I was. I said I was a real estate agent looking for a small ranch for a California client, and I had heard his was to be auctioned off. I used my lowest voice tones and a cool, businesslike approach. There are more than one or two actresses in the family. Or good liars.

There was a long pause while the banker switched me to someone else, who asked me to wait. Finally a woman came on and said that proceedings were under way, and the time and place of the auction would be published in the newspapers. We thanked each other and said good-bye.

Aha! We'd be rid of our gun-toting, gate-smashing neighbor. We could watch the papers for the notice. He'd probably be gone before the actual auction anyway, wouldn't he? Did the ex-owners usually hang around to cry at their funerals? I shouldn't think so.

I hoped it would be soon. What worried me most was fire. There are always a lot of lightning-started forest fires around the state, especially in late summer and fall, when it's dry. It would be easy for Sawyer or whoever to start a fire near our place. Forest fires are a fear for every northwesterner.

The morning dragged by. On the noon news Dapper Dan said that Hobart Sawyer was out on bail, just as Mom said he would be. That was bad. They didn't mention "the juvenile," who had to be that slimy Donny who worked for Sawyer, but he was probably out too.

When I figured Nonny would be up, I dialed her number. Sarah, her longtime secretary, answered as she always does, and we had a brief chat. Sarah is a sweetheart, and she's probably the only one in the world who could take care of Nonny and her affairs without ever getting ruffled.

When Nonny came on, I told her about Savannah's getting a real part in the last show of the season. She was pleased.

"Darling, I had decided to come for a visit anyway, but this makes it all the better. Sarah has made plane reservations for me. Do you have a pencil?"

I pulled my faithful Pilot Extra Fine from my pocket and grabbed the memo pad. "Fire when ready."

She gave me time and day of departure, airline, flight number, and time of arrival at Missoula.

"If you can't meet me, don't worry. I'll take a cab."

"Of course we'll meet you. Nonny, it's a two-hour drive. Where do you want to stay? I'll make a reservation." Our place was too small, but anyway she always liked to stay at a hotel.

"Some decent hotel that's not too far from you. Only, darling, not a dude ranch."

I laughed. "I promise. No cowboys."

"Well, it isn't the cowboys so much; it's the cows."

"Nonny, I can't wait to see you."

"Nor I you. But Lee . . ." She hesitated, which alarmed me. Nonny never hesitates, whether she's talking or moving.

137

"What is it, Nonny?"

"Darling, I'm older. Since you saw me, I've grown older."

I laughed with relief. Typical actor's worry. "We're all older, Nonny. I'm almost as tall as you now, and Savannah is growing up very fast."

"At your age it's fun. At my age it isn't."

"You could never be old."

"Well"—she gave a little laugh—"hold that thought. And let's keep my visit a secret until a few days before I leave, shall we?"

"Great."

"You might check with me three or four days before my arrival, to make sure everything is shipshape. Then that night I'll call the family and spring the surprise."

When I hung up, I practically danced out to see the wolves.

"You'll never guess," I told them, "who's coming to see you!"

CHAPTER 28

The story about the smashing of our fence was in the paper, not because it was such a big event in itself but because it involved wolves, and that was a hot topic. Then there were more letters to the editor, for and against, and Dad said there had been calls to the station.

The next day I saw Donny the Creep downtown. It was the first time I'd seen him since the fence smashing. He was driving Sawyer's old pickup, and he leaned out the window and yelled, "Wolf lover!" at me in a triumphant voice.

A young man in jeans and a baseball cap yelled back at him, "Go soak your head, Donny!"

"Thanks," I said.

"I'm thinking of organizing a group for the extermination of human vermin," the man said. And he climbed on a motorcycle and rode off. To this day I don't know who he was, but I consider him a friend.

I was trying to get a good first chapter on my wolf book, but I had done it over about twenty times. I never knew it was so hard to get writing right.

Of course I was also spending a lot of time cueing my sister, and poor Mom was back in the chauffeur business, taking Savannah to rehearsals and picking her up. I wondered if she might really go back to California with Nonny, and how I would feel about it if she did. Nobody had said anything definite, but it seemed to be in the air.

The day before Savannah's birthday I went to Kalispell with Dad to get her a present. Also I wanted to have a look at the hotel rooms I'd reserved for Nonny. They hadn't had a suite, so I'd taken two connecting rooms. The clerk took me upstairs to see them. They were pleasant enough, and there was a great view of the mountains. No cows, Nonny!

I got Savannah a little silver whistle on a silver chain. Mom worried about Savannah, as young as she was, being around sophisticated people, and being so pretty. She was concerned about guys coming on to her. Personally I thought Savannah could handle it; she had a fantastic scream. But anyway now she could blow her whistle.

Dad took me to lunch, and I hung around the studio for a while, watching what they did in the control room and behind the scenes.

Then I went out to a pay phone and called Nonny collect. It was about time for her to notify the family that she was coming.

She had made a surprising change in plans. "Sweetheart, don't meet me at the airport. Sarah has made arrangements with a limo service for a man and a car to drive me to the hotel and stay with me while I'm there. I can't have your mother driving back and forth to Kalispell all the time to pick me up and take me back. Besides, I might want to do a spot of exploring, Glacier Park for instance."

I couldn't believe she didn't want us to meet her. I told her we'd love to. "It's no trouble at all. Savannah has a dress rehearsal that night, but the rest of us can come."

"No, dear, it's all arranged. I'll sleep off my jet lag at the hotel and have the driver bring me to you the next day."

I thought she sounded tired, but she insisted she was fine. She would call the family that evening. "Till then, love."

On our way home Dad said, "I've made a deal with a fellow about putting in metal gates on the road and at the enclosure, and some kind of alarm system, like one of those sirens some people have in their cars for burglar alarms. He'll get at it the first of the week if he can. Which probably means next month."

"Good." Maybe I could sleep through the night without waking up every few hours thinking I heard someone.

Dad had cleaned up the broken gate and taken it to the dump in the pickup. There was nothing now to make anyone even hesitate about coming on in. A couple of tight-lipped guys had come to look, making no comment. And I hated having to tell curious families with kids that we were sorry but we couldn't let them into the enclosure, and the wolves were hidden in the forest anyway. One kid cried all the way back to their car, and I felt like a heel.

"You know," Mom said, "if we still have the wolves, and Silver has pups, it would be nice to take one of the young ones around to the schools, when it's old enough, to let the children see how undangerous they are."

If we still had the wolves? But I liked the school idea.

I spent a lot of time with the wolves, partly to escape having to cue Savannah when she was home, but mostly because I loved to be with them. They were beginning to look very handsome as their coats filled out, shiny and thick. Even my beloved Ruthie looked like a real wolf now. I loved her coat of many colors. Once when I went out there, she was actually playing with Silver. I couldn't believe it. Of course Silver made it clear that she was boss, but they were having fun.

I couldn't wait for Nonny to see them.

CHAPTER 29

That night Nonny called with her surprise, and our cabin was practically bursting its walls with the excitement. We never said that I had known about it, but Mom remembered our phone conversation, and she gave me a knowing look.

Savannah had that evening off, with a run-through scheduled for the next night. She was practically hysterical about Nonny's coming. She was thrilled that Nonny would see her performance, but terrified that she wouldn't do well enough. Mom spent an hour trying to calm her down, while Dad fussed over the fact that Nonny did not want us to meet her. That seemed all wrong to him.

"It's not hospitality, let alone tender loving care, letting her come into that little airport all alone and get driven up here by some godforsaken limo that'll probably turn out to be a '78 Ford, and who knows what the driver will be. She's a famous woman. He might even rob her or something."

He finally persuaded Mom, against her better judgment (and against mine, if anybody had been listening to me), that we should meet her, hug her, make her welcome, and check out this limo business. If Dad thought it looked okay, and she still wanted to use it, fine. If not, we were there to bring her north.

Savannah couldn't go because of her dress rehearsal, and she moaned and groaned about that, but I thought it was a good thing. If Nonny did change her mind (which she seldom did, once she'd made it up), it would have been very crowded in Mom's car with all of us.

The next day Mom and I cleaned house. I brushed the wolves' coats till they shone. Mom cooked and shopped, and Dad brought home a bottle of expensive champagne, the kind Nonny likes. He had to go check out the hotel rooms too. Sometimes I think he cares more about Nonny than about all of us put together. Maybe because she's a celebrity.

On the big night we drove Savannah to the theater; Mom arranged with the wardrobe mistress to keep her if we didn't get back before the rehearsal was over, and off we went, much earlier than we needed to.

We had hamburgers at the Bar MG and settled down in the little Missoula airport to wait. And wait.

The plane from Spokane, where Nonny had to change, was almost an hour and a half late. Nothing is more boring than waiting in an airport. I was wishing we had done what she said, or at least had phoned ahead to see if the plane was on time. There was no limo and chauffeur in sight. He'd probably had sense enough to call.

When Dad went to ask the reservations clerk for the forty-fourth time (give or take), the clerk grinned and said, "Six minutes, sir."

I did my cowboy yell, and Mom rushed to the ladies' room to comb her hair and fix her lipstick. We went over to gate four, through the check-your-bombs line, and waited. You can't see the field from there, but in a few minutes we heard the plane. I felt almost sick with excitement. Mom looked pale, and Dad was teetering up and down. There were only a few people waiting, but then lo! there was a man in a brown suit and a chauffeur's cap that said BIG SKY LIMOUSINE INC. in tiny gold letters above the visor. He stood apart from all of us, looking bored. Dad looked him over and started to go speak to him, but Mom stopped him.

You could hear the plane circling the airfield, and then the whoosh it made when it came in for a landing.

A young woman in an airline uniform appeared and opened the door where the steps come up from the field. I had an awful feeling that since Nonny wasn't expecting us, she might not be pleased. She likes to know ahead of time what she's getting into. I do too, so I understand that. Mom looked anxious too. But Dad was beaming from ear to ear. I heard him tell someone his mother-in-law was on the plane.

"From California. Savannah Saxton. You've probably seen her on the screen."

Mom gave him an angry nudge. Poor Dad—what'll he do if his own Savannah makes it to celebrity?

The limo guy stopped leaning against the wall and came to attention.

A young couple came running up the steps and ran off

with two guys. An older man came more slowly and stopped to catch his breath. Two more people came up the steps, then a middle-aged couple complaining about the cold night air. Montana nights are always cold, so they had to be tourists.

Nobody else came, but the attendant was still standing there.

"Maybe she missed the connection," Dad said.

"She's usually one of the first off." Mom sounded worried.

Dad went up to the attendant. "Any more passengers? We're expecting"—he glanced at Mom—"my wife's mother."

She looked at her clipboard. "One more."

We waited. Even the limo man was looking nervous. He was probably wondering if he'd met the wrong plane.

Then there she was. She didn't see us, because she was looking down, walking carefully up the step. A flight attendant was trying to help her. Nonny smiled and shook her off, but the way she was walking! Slow and a little bent over, and she had a cane! Of course it was a beautiful cane, painted dark red with some kind of tiny figures in black all over it, and the handle was a carved eagle's head.

None of us moved or spoke for a moment. Then, as she stood in the doorway catching her breath, she looked up. On her left eye she was wearing an eye patch, the same red as the cane, with tiny seed pearls all over it.

"Mother!" Mom's voice trembled.

Nonny looked up sharply and frowned. "I was not to be met." Her voice sounded cold and angry. She looked accusingly at me.

146

"Lee told us." Mom went up to her and hugged her in a quick nervous way, as if Nonny might break. "We just wanted to say hello. . . ."

Nonny softened. "Of course. How nice!" She gave Mom a proper hug, and then Dad and me. "How wonderful to see you." She was standing up straight now, looking more like herself. The actress.

She lifted her head and saw the limo man and nodded. "I have a limo, you see. I thought tomorrow we could have a proper reunion." She made a face. "That plane! It's like riding a buzzing hornet."

The limo man said, "I'll get your luggage, madam, if you'll give me your checks." He took the whole ticket from her hands as she fumbled with it, removed the baggage checks, and went over to the luggage conveyor, which was already moving.

"How are you?" It was the first thing Dad had said. He sounded scared, somehow.

"Oh, wonderful." She was holding her head high, like the old Nonny I knew. "Just a bit of nuisance with this eye. The silly patch slows me down for the moment. How do you like it? Chic, isn't it?" She laughed her throaty stage laugh.

"It's a beauty," Dad said, "and I love that cane. Custom made, I'll bet."

"Oh, of course." She was holding my hand now, and I felt a little better. She wasn't mad at me. "An old friend of mine had it made. Those are Aztec figures. Aren't they delightful?"

She chattered like that till the limo man came. "The luggage is in the car, madam," he said. "If you're ready . . ."

"Yes, indeed. I'll see you all tomorrow, darlings. I suppose Savannah is rehearsing?"

"Dress rehearsal," Dad said. "She was heartbroken not to come."

"All in good time." She gave us a little wave and walked away with the limo guy, though she shook her head when he tried to take her arm. She was walking with her back straight and her usual springy step. But just at the door to the parking lot, she stumbled. He caught her, and held the door. And they were gone.

"It's just the patch," Mom said. "Remember when you got hit in the eye by a baseball, Lee, and had to wear one? She's getting new contacts."

Mom was whistling in the dark. Nonny looked old and tired. And you don't wear an eye patch just to get new contacts. Something was wrong.

CHAPTER 30

The person Nonny confided in about her eye was me. She stayed in bed most of the day after she came, and then Dad went and got her. She wanted to come in the limo, but Dad persuaded her it was no road for a limo, so she gave Eric the evening off, telling him he should come later to the theater.

She and Dad came just before Savannah had to leave for the big opening-night hoopla. Between seeing Nonny and then having to leave, and opening-night nerves, Savannah was, as they say, beside herself. (Which I always think is a funny expression. I see two hysterical Savannahs, side by side.)

Nonny had said for us to have a light supper because she had arranged a party after the opening. It would be on the set, for the whole company. Efficient Nonny had gotten in touch with the director, who of course was out of his mind with joy at having Savannah Saxton come to his play. The party was to be a surprise for everybody else though. Not even Savannah knew about it.

Nonny looked more rested. She was wearing her version of small-western-town opening-night dress: perfectly tailored pale pink slacks and a matching pink silk shirt, with a beautiful handmade white shawl for the evening chill. And of course the fancy eye patch. When Mom tried to find out more about that, Nonny brushed her off.

But later when I took her out to see the wolves, she told me.

"I don't want them fussing about it while I'm here. I want everything to be happy. But just between us, it's not exactly serendipitous. What I thought was a simple cataract, and they just laser them off these days, you know, nothing to it . . . well, it turned out to be something called wet macular degeneration. Doesn't that sound revolting?"

"What is it?" I felt scared.

"When you reach"—she paused and grinned her wonderful, mischievous grin that had enchanted audiences for years—"a *certain age*, the blood vessels behind the eye get lazy, and the body sends in new ones, but they don't bother to rehearse these new chaps, so they do all the wrong things. Some of them piled up in my eye, at the back where the film would be in a camera, and they bled. Well, the stupid asses bled all over my macula, so I've lost the vision in that eye."

I was shocked. "Forever?"

"Forever. Except for the side. I can see things out of the corner of my eye, as they say. It's annoying."

She was sounding so casual, it scared me all the more. "Can it happen to the other eye?"

She waved her hand in one of her famous gestures. "Oh, it could, but we are keeping careful track. If it starts outside the macula, it can be just lasered away."

I caught her hand. "Nonny, stop acting. It's serious, isn't it."

In a different, quiet voice she said, "It's a nasty problem, but it's not going to kill me or anything. I just don't care for the idea of being blind, even half blind." Then she changed her voice again, to cheerful. "Now where are your wolves?"

"Nonny . . ." I was almost crying.

"Darling Lee," she said, "you're the one I tell these things to, because you know and I know that bad things can happen and one deals with them as best one can. You're the only one in the family who really understands that. I don't know where you got it . . . maybe you were born with it. But it's why I count on you."

I guess nobody ever said anything that meant more to me in my whole life. I have written it down, and I will never forget it, especially when bad things happen.

We went into the enclosure, and the wolves came out to meet us. Nonny was really overcome by how beautiful they are. It was not an act; she really reacted to them the way I do. She wanted to know each one's name, and in no time she had all of them but Ruthie pushing their noses at her, getting to know her. I had to fend them off so they wouldn't get her clothes dirty.

"Tomorrow I'm coming out here in jeans," she said, "and sneakers, so we can really get acquainted. Oh, Lee, they're so handsome. Those eyes! Where on earth could the myth of big bad wolf have come from?" She tried to coax Ruthie closer. "She's not really one of them, is she?"

"No, but they're not as mean to her as they used to be. Snow plays with her, and even Silver sometimes, but, of course, they're the boss."

"How like humans!"

Mom called us in to supper, and Nonny had to hear again the story of Arthur Washington, whom she remembered as a very young man trying to break into show business.

Then it was time to leave for the theater. All of us were nervous for Savannah. It was hard on her to play her first real part with Nonny in the audience. I hoped it wouldn't make her too jittery. I was jittery myself about the wolves. Everyone would know we were leaving them alone.

"I should have thought," Nonny said. "It would have been better not to let Savannah know I was here till after the opening."

"Oh, she'll do fine," Dad said, but he kept sliding his watch bracelet up and down his wrist the way he did when he was nervous.

Actually, we needn't have worried. From her first entrance right through her last scene, she was poised and beautiful and very, very good. I was more than proud of her; I felt a kind of admiration and love for her that I'd never dreamed of feeling for my pesky kid sister. I wasn't sure it would last. I'd been to enough plays to know that sometimes you react to the part and forget the real person. Just the same, this younger Savannah was something special.

During the final applause and the curtain calls, I looked at Nonny. She had lifted her eye patch just a little and was dabbing at her eye. Tears? I wasn't sure. She fixed the patch in place and began applauding with hard, loud claps. Then she stood up, clapping, and a lot of other people followed. In seconds the whole house was standing and cheering. Of course it wasn't just for my sister. It was a good play, and everyone had done very well. They were mostly people from the university drama department.

Camera flashbulbs were popping, aimed at the stage and more than a few finding Nonny. She smiled and shook her head, waving toward the cast.

When the house had cleared, the stage manager rang up the curtain, and the director told everybody they were having a party. He got Nonny onstage and presented her. Nonny and Savannah had their arms around each other. My mother was smiling and crying. My dad had a grin from one of his big ears to the other.

Nonny had hired a caterer, and it was probably the grandest party that theater had ever had. I got myself a plate of food and went to sit in one of the front-row seats. The house was dark, so I felt private, and I could watch everything. I felt kind of lonely, but writers are supposed to be watchers.

When I had almost finished the last tiny crab salad sandwich, someone came up behind me and said, "*Aloha,* Ms. Lee."

I was surprised at how glad I was to see Bryan. He put one long leg over the seat backs and then the other, and sat down beside me.

"She did fine," he said.

"Yes. She did. You saw the show, I guess?" Silly question.

"Most of it. I've been working in the box office for the last two weeks."

"Oh! I didn't see you."

"Nobody notices the box office guy." He laughed. "Not a bad job though. I grab 'em where I find 'em. I'm going to take some courses at the community college this fall, so I need moola. *Ha na—ha na* . . . work work."

We talked quite a while, and he asked me to go out in the catamaran on Sunday, if the weather was good. By the time he left, I felt a lot better. If he was going to the college, he must be maybe seventeen. My man from Hawaii! Ha! And Savannah didn't even know about us. The secret, mysterious life of Lee McDougall. Tune in next week.

CHAPTER 31

The next morning my sister the star was super impossible. She slept late, of course, which you could forgive, but when she got up, it was, "Mom, did you press my costume?" "Lee, will you find my second-act scarf? It's here somewhere." And so on.

"Why didn't you leave your costume at the theater?" I said. "It's very unprofessional to run around in public in costume."

"I happened to be very fatigued," she said coldly, stringing out the "fatigued" into six syllables. "Would you get me a glass of milk?" She was having breakfast, eating like a horse for a great actress who was so faaa-tiggg-ued.

"Get your own milk," I said.

She started to yell at me, but Mom came on strong.

"Savannah," she said, "you played a small part last night

in an amateur production. You did very nicely, but it does not turn you into Sarah Bernhardt or the queen of this household. You can press your own costume, find your own scarf, and get your own milk. Neither Lee nor I are your slaves."

Savannah burst into tears, then stopped, remembering it would make her face red and swollen for the performance. Instead she said, under her breath, a four-letter word that is not allowed in our house and slammed into her room.

Mom was there in two seconds, jerking the door open. "If you ever speak to me like that again, I will take you out of this play and all future plays."

"You couldn't do that." Savannah sounded alarmed.

"Watch me," Mom said, and slammed the door.

In the kitchen she said, "One prima donna in a lifetime is enough."

I decided it was a good time to go out and see the wolves. I had been working on a drawing of Ruthie that was coming along well. I played with all of them for a while, and then sat down beside Ruthie with my sketch pad. She was lying down facing me, her head on her paws, those warm intelligent eyes watching to see what I was up to.

Snow came over and tried to push my pencil out of my hand, but I shooed him away and he went off to pester Thunder. Silver stood just behind me and watched me draw, as if she was really interested.

"You see," I told her, "Ruthie's got a lot going for her that you haven't appreciated. If you have pups next year, you're going to be glad to have Aunt Ruthie's help. And don't forget, if your Arthur Washington hadn't heard about

Ruthie, you might be in some awful zoo somewhere, or even dead."

Ruthie flicked her ears forward whenever I said her name. And almost as if she had understood, Silver went over to Ruthie and sniffed her neck. Ruthie didn't move. Silver gave her a playful little nudge and went off to flirt with Thunder. The vet who had given Ruthie her rabies shot said that wolves began thinking of courtship about this time of year. I wonder how come humans think about it all year round.

Soon after Mom had driven Savannah off for her spot rehearsals, Nonny hollered hello and came wearing an old pair of jeans and a blue sweatshirt that would have matched her eyes if she hadn't been wearing wraparound dark glasses.

I was surprised to see her. Did she travel with old jeans and beat-up sneakers? "Hi. How'd you get here?"

"Eric drove me as far as the turnoff, and I walked in." She had her cane, but she wasn't wearing her eye patch, obviously. She dropped down on the grass beside me and looked at my drawing. "Lee, you are getting very good. I mean it. Your mother mentioned a book you might be doing about the wolves, a picture book?"

"I think it's turning into a longer book. But I'm only on a very rough draft. Ruthie is the heroine."

"Of course." She ruffled Snow's neck fur. He and Silver were nuzzling her shoulders, and Thunder, usually so aloof, was pulling at her green sneakers.

She put her arm around Silver's neck. "How is Vannie today?"

"Impossible."

She laughed. "Morning after."

"She's a twelve-year-old kid playing one small part in a little summer theater, and she thinks she's the new Meryl Streep."

"Or the new Savannah Saxton? In this morning's paper she got one word. It said: 'Promising.' No, she's no Meryl Streep, but I think she has possibilities." She picked a long blade of grass, put it between her thumbs, and whistled. The wolves loved it. "That's one of the gifts I'm proudest of," she told Thunder. And then she said, "Lee, I came late on purpose, to find you alone. I want to take Savannah home with me."

"For a visit?"

"To live. With all of you coming out for Christmases, and Savannah coming here for the summers. What do you think?"

It was a shock, even though Savannah had mentioned it, and I knew Nonny had thought of it. "Why?"

"Aside from seeing all of you, I came this time to see if she has talent. If she stays here, she'll go on being big actress frog in small theatrical puddle. She'll be overpraised and spoiled. You'll resent her, and she will never be a real actress."

I didn't know what to say. As many times as I had wished it, I couldn't imagine Savannah gone.

"My acting career is over. Half-blind, unsteady old girls are not in great demand. But I can teach, the way I learned from Stella Adler. I think I have a lot to give young beginners." She paused. "I've already signed up four youngsters."

"Where would Savannah go to school?"

"We have excellent schools. That's no problem. The

child has talent, Lee, and she ought to have a chance to work at it. I began when I was five."

"Maybe she's too old." I wanted to lighten up the conversation so I could handle it.

She smiled. "She needs to find out what hard work is in the theater. She needs to be disappointed often. She needs to know what it's like to fail."

"That takes a lot of strength, Nonny. You have it. Does Savannah?"

"I think so, but if not, we'll soon find out." She stretched her long legs out. "I need your opinion."

I stood up. "No, you don't, Nonny. I'm only two years older than Savannah. How would I know what's good for her? How do I know what Mom would feel about it, or Dad?"

She looked startled. "I think I've always thought of you as the wise and sensible one. You've been many places, you've been uprooted over and over, and you have survived it. You have coped so well. . . . You seem grown-up."

"Savannah's traveled everywhere I have." I felt very upset. Nonny was talking about breaking up our family. "I'm not grown-up. I have trouble enough running my own life." I felt as if she had used me, all that secret stuff.

She pushed the wolves away and stood up. "I've upset you. I'm sorry."

I could tell I had hurt her feelings. I tried to lighten up.

"You aren't wearing your beautiful eye patch."

"I wear it for focusing. Reading on the plane or watching a play. Otherwise my eyes send conflicting messages to my brain and confuse it." She gave a sad little laugh. "Heaven

knows my brain is confused enough without adding to it."
She started walking toward the house.

But you wore it all through the party, I thought, and all the time you were here. Because it attracts attention. In a weird way it's glamorous.

Then I felt really ashamed of myself. I was criticizing Nonny for being who she was, who she had always been, my grandmother the actress whom I adored.

I ran after her. "Mom's got this wonderful tea made from flowers, a touch of cinnamon. Would you like some?" I put my arm around her. She felt awfully thin.

She leaned her head against mine for a second. "I'd love it."

So we drank flowery tea and talked about old times in Laguna Beach, and when Mom came home, I got my bike and left. I didn't want to hear Nonny asking Mom about taking Savannah away.

CHAPTER 32

I stayed out of the way for a while and let the storm rage over whether Savannah should go with Nonny or not. Savannah herself had moments of terror at the idea of leaving home, but most of the time she could hardly wait to go. She saw herself starring in a sitcom by next year at the latest. Little did she know about Nonny's "learning to fail" theory. I'd have to remember that myself when I really got into writing books. Rejections, I guess, everybody got.

My dad was pretty upset about Savannah's leaving, but also he was proud. He too saw her as starring practically right away. My daughter the movie star. I wondered if he'd ever brag about his daughter the writer.

Nonny was staying over another week after the play closed to give everybody a chance to get used to Savannah's leaving, and to give her time to pack.

So almost without anyone making a final decision, it was settled: Savannah would go.

Nonny's chauffeur took them all on a trip through Glacier Park the day I went out in the catamaran with Bryan. Savannah was impressed that he had asked me.

"He must be at least seventeen," she said.

"I like old men," I told her, and she laughed. We were being very nice to each other for a change.

Skimming along the lake in the beautiful boat with its bright striped sails was the most peaceful time I'd had in ages. Later Bryan took down the sail, and we drifted along the shoreline as the afternoon got hotter and the breeze died down.

He showed me the boathouse where he lived, and we sat on the dock and ate hot dogs broiled on a little hibachi, and drank lemonade. He was easy to talk to. He told me a lot about Hawaii.

I hated to leave, but I wanted to get home before the family did so my father wouldn't start stewing about "Lee being out with strange men"—even though Mom told him she'd met Bryan.

They got back about twenty minutes after I did, full of stories about mountain goats and bears and gorgeous scenery, and the Going to the Sun Highway, which gave Nonny vertigo. They seemed to have had a really good time. Savannah had developed a small crush on Eric, who was a law school student and "really cute without his chauffeur cap on." I wondered if Nonny knew what she was getting into, having Savannah full-time.

The next morning Mom took Savannah to Kalispell to shop. Mom wasn't happy about leaving me home alone.

She worried because of the arguments going on around town about our wolves, and she especially worried about Sawyer. But I persuaded her I'd be fine.

An hour after they'd gone I heard a truck drive up and stop out where the gate had been. My heart began to pound. I wished I had the gun that was in Dad's pickup, even if it wasn't loaded.

I was scared to go look, but when nobody came, and then I heard hammering, I realized it must be the man with the new gate. I crossed my fingers and went to see.

Two of them were hammering steel posts into the ground. They were friendly. The man in charge showed me the shiny new gate.

"Put a padlock on 'er at night, and nobody's going to drive through there."

" 'Course they could get out and walk around it," the younger guy said, grinning. "If they didn't mind getting scratched up some."

"Mr. McDougall's ordered two of them siren alarms, for here and for the gate where the wolves are. You tell him they haven't come yet, but I'll bring 'em out soon as they come in."

"Guess they're auctioning off Sawyer's place," the younger one said. "We got stuck behind half a dozen pickups and vans on the way in."

"It was advertised in the paper," the older man said.

I could have yelled for joy. Why hadn't I seen it?

"Guess you won't mind seein' him go," the young one said. "He busted in your other gate, I heard. Got him up on charges."

"You can bet old Hobie'll be long gone before the

hearing," the older man said. "And the law's not going to chase him for a busted gate."

I got my bike and started over there. I'd never gone down that road, but I thought I could probably keep out of sight if there were a bunch of people around. I wanted to see for myself that Sawyer was really gone. We'd all sleep better.

It was only about a mile down the trail. About a half dozen pickups and four-wheel drives were parked any old way near the place. I could see the auctioneer, but he seemed to be getting ready to leave. It was not much of a house. The roof sagged, and the place needed paint.

One man passed me on the way to his Blazer. "You're too late, young lady, if you wanted to buy a two-bit, no-account ranch that ain't big enough for six sheep. She's already gone to the highest bidder." He gave me a big grin and swung into the cab of the Blazer.

I moved a little closer, keeping on the other side of the road, where there were plenty of trees. I watched the auctioneer go away in a van. People were drifting off. At first I didn't see Sawyer, and I began to think he wasn't there, but then I saw him come out of the house and sink down onto the steps with his head in his hands. Three other men gathered around him, passing a bottle around. One of them seemed to be trying to comfort Sawyer. For the first time I almost felt sorry for him. It must be awful to have all your property sold out from under you, even if it was "no-account." I wondered where the sheep were. Maybe they went with the place.

A middle-aged woman came across the road to a pickup

parked near me. She was tall and thin and wore jeans tucked into boots. She was very tanned.

"Hello." She gave me a nice smile. "Auction's over."

"Who bought it?"

"Some organization. I never did hear who it was."

Organization! I hoped it wasn't some weirdo cult. There were several around the state, and they always seemed to be in trouble with their neighbors.

"Might have been those people who buy up land to preserve it, I'm not sure. You live around here?"

"Next door."

She opened the pickup door and sat on the seat with her legs out. "Say! Would you be the girl with the wolves?"

I said I was, and she got quite excited.

"That must be wonderful. I've thought about doing something like that myself. I've raised Arabians for years, but I broke my hip a while back—got thrown from my favorite horse, can you believe it? She stepped in a hole. Broke her leg, beyond fixing. I had to have her put down." She paused.

"I'm sorry." She looked so sad, I didn't really know what to say.

"Well, that's life. But it took the heart out of me. And I'm not too good in the saddle anymore, so we sold the rest of the horses. But I need something."

"You'd love wolves. They're great."

"I believe I'll look into it."

Her husband came across the road. She introduced us and told him about the wolves.

He looked back at the men on the steps. I looked too

and saw Donny. He had seen me and was shouting some-thing.

"Why don't we just put your bike in the back here," the man said, "and give you a lift home."

All those men were looking at me now. I was very glad to get into the pickup. The woman said her name was Mamie Taylor, and her husband was Charlie.

"Hobie's pretty cut up," Charlie Taylor said, "and like always, he's looking for somebody to blame."

"Always did," Mamie said. "I went to school with his wife. She finally couldn't stand any more of him and took off a couple of years ago. Forty-eight years old and ran off with a handsome Salish, went to California." She laughed. "Tickled me to death that she got up the gumption. I got a Christmas card from her last year. Living in some little town near San Diego, happy as a lark."

"Good for her!" It made me feel good that that woman had escaped.

I showed Charlie Taylor where to turn off to our place. The men putting in the gates had gone. I explained about Sawyer smashing the old gate.

"Anybody home at your house?" Charlie Taylor asked me.

"Not right now. But they'll be home soon. My mom and sister went shopping."

"If you don't mind," he said, "why don't we just sit around and shoot the breeze till they get back? Hobie's in a bad mood."

I was really touched and very relieved that they would do that. I took them out and showed them the wolves, and we stayed out there quite a while, talking about Ruthie and how I came to have the pack.

When my mother and Savannah came home, Nonny was with them. They invited the Taylors in for a cup of tea, and it was really nice. Of course it turned out that Nonny knew someone in California who raised Arabians.

By the time the Taylors left, we were all friends, and we'd exchanged phone numbers and addresses and promises to keep in touch.

Soon after they left, Dad came home, and I began to relax.

CHAPTER 33

That night Nonny came to have dinner with us. I hadn't seen her alone since the talk we'd had about Savannah's going. But when I went out to feed the wolves, she followed me.

She seemed really to enjoy the wolves and she remembered their names and personalities. She watched as I tossed the chunks of meat over the fence, and first Thunder, then Silver, and finally Snow and Prometheus grabbed their dinner, Snow always giving way a little if Prometheus insisted.

Ruthie stood off to the side waiting.

Nonny nodded toward her. "Poor Ruthie. Low wolf on the totem pole."

"It's better than it used to be. They aren't so mean about driving her away. I used to have to wait and throw hers off to her separately after the others were through. I keep hoping that someday they'll let her really be part of the family."

We watched as she sidled in, head low, and snatched a piece of meat almost from under Snow's nose. He growled, but he didn't make a thing of it. There was another big piece for him to tear into.

"Lee," Nonny said, "you aren't still angry with me, are you?"

"Nonny!" I wished she didn't have on those blasted dark glasses. I wanted to see her eyes. "Of course I'm not. I wasn't angry with you then. I just . . . I don't know . . . it's hard being the sister of a beautiful, talented person like Savannah. I guess I was just trying to protect myself."

She put her arm around me. "I couldn't stand it if you and I lost any of our close friendship."

I hugged her. "We never could. Never."

"I really think I'm doing the right thing for Savannah. She is so much like me, I think I understand her. If she never gets her chance, she'll be bitter and sad. And an actor can't start too soon."

"I know she'll be fine." I looked at the funny little designs on Nonny's cane and thought of my sister surrounded by actors and writers, people like Arthur Washington. She'd be somebody different the next time I saw her. "I'll miss her."

"We'll be in close touch."

I looked at the dark glasses and the cane. "And let Savannah help you, Nonny. She needs to learn to be considerate."

She smiled. "Thank you, dear. Yes, I'll need help."

That wasn't what I had said, but Nonny always reads me right. It hurt to know Nonny would need help.

Dad took her back to her hotel at about eleven o'clock.

Savannah said afterward that she was still awake when she heard a sound. The rest of us were asleep, so she got up and went into the kitchen and turned on the yard lights. Then she screamed and ran out of the house.

I don't remember the order that things happened in, but by the time I got to the kitchen, Mom was on the phone, Dad was running out, still pulling on his pants, and shadowy men were racing across our clearing. Dad went after them.

I found Savannah inside the wolf enclosure, frantically pushing the wolves away from the fence and throwing hunks of meat over the fence. I was so startled to see Savannah, who was terrified of wolves, right in there pushing them around, I stopped short for an instant.

"Get in here!" she yelled. "Get this meat out. It's poisoned!"

I got there fast. The wolves were trying hard to get at the stuff, and once I literally tore a piece out of Snow's mouth.

When we had thrown the last piece over the fence, and Savannah had poked around to make sure there was none left, I said, "How do you know it was poisoned?"

"One of them yelled, 'Let 'em choke on that!' " She was breathing hard. Silver pushed at her knees, and almost absently Savannah reached down and stroked her head. Then she looked at me and said, "What am I doing? I'm terrified of wolves."

"Not anymore. You saved their lives."

Mom came in with her big flashlight. I told her what had happened, and she said the police were on the way. She gave Savannah a surprised look and said, "You saved them, Vannie."

I was counting the wolves. "Where's Ruthie?" I searched the bushes nearby. "Was she here with the others, Van?"

"I don't know. I can't tell them apart. Anyway I didn't have time to count. I had to get the meat away from them and throw it over the fence."

I took Mom's flashlight and went to look for Ruthie.

CHAPTER 34

The forest was very dark and cold. I went first to her den, but she wasn't there. I could hear Mom and Savannah calling her, and I saw the flashes of their lights.

I remember when our cat was sick, he went off by himself to die, and it took forever to find him. But Ruthie wouldn't die. She had just been scared off by all the noise and confusion. And if the other wolves were growling at Savannah, Ruthie would think it was meant for her.

"Ruthie," I kept calling. "It's all right. Come on out. Everybody's going to get special, good meat for a treat. Come on out, Ruthie."

Then I began to get a little impatient with her. This

was ridiculous. She knew I was her friend; I'd look after her.

The other wolves were huddled together in the clearing. They hadn't figured out what was going on: Somebody had offered them meat, and then their own people had taken it away.

Through the trees I could see flashing police lights. I didn't know whether Dad had caught any of the men or not. He's very fast on his feet, and he doesn't scare easily.

"Ruthie," I kept calling. "Come on. Quit hiding."

"Lee." It was my mother's voice, a little way off, down by the dry bed of the little stream. "I've found her."

I fell down twice, trying to run in the dark. I could see Mom's outline, bending over the creek bed, and I heard Savannah crashing through the woods toward us.

Ruthie lay very still on the pebbly creek bottom. She had vomited. Mom was feeling for her heartbeat.

"She's alive, but just barely." She pulled off her sweater and wrapped it around Ruthie. "We have to get her to the vet fast. Lee, help me carry her. Van, go call the vet. The number is on the pad by the phone. Keep calling till he wakes up, and tell him to meet us at the clinic right away. Life or death."

Ruthie tried to lift her head, then let it fall back. For a moment I thought she had died, but she looked at me. Her eyes were glazed, and I don't know if she really saw me.

We carried Ruthie as gently as we could and put her in the backseat of Mom's car. Dad and the police car were gone. I could see Savannah on the phone in the kitchen.

As Mom turned the car around, Savannah came tearing out of the house and pushed in beside me on the front seat. "He'll be there."

"Good." I suddenly felt calm. We'd found Ruthie, she was still alive, and the vet would take care of her. Everything would be all right.

CHAPTER 35

Ruthie lay motionless on the vet's examining table while he checked her all over.

"Does she hurt?" Savannah asked.

"She's in shock. Why don't you folks go home now. I'll do everything I can."

"I tried to get all the meat away from them." Savannah was white-faced and shaking.

Mom put her arm around her. "You were very brave, honey. You did fine. Dr. Nash, you'll call us?"

"You bet."

Nobody spoke on the way home. Mom tried to get us to go to bed, but we didn't. We sat in the kitchen near the phone.

Dad came home, looking grim. "The police got one of the guys, but not Sawyer. He was the one who organized it. They're out looking for him. They picked up that Donny kid, but he swears he wasn't there."

Mom scrambled some eggs and made coffee and hot chocolate, but nobody ate much. I had stopped feeling that Ruthie would be all right. Every minute that went by without the phone ringing scared me worse.

The wolves began to bark. They almost never did that without some reason. Dad went out to make sure they were all right. He fed them, and they quieted down. But every once in a while one of them would howl. I wasn't sure which one it was, but I thought it was Silver. I wished I could tell Ruthie that Silver was worried about her.

The sun was just coming up when Dr. Nash called. Ruthie was dead.

CHAPTER 36

The next day, the last day of Nonny's visit, she took me to lunch, alone, in a small restaurant in Bigfork. We went late, so it wasn't crowded with tourists, and we sat in a booth at the back. It was dark enough for Nonny to take off her sunglasses. I realized it was the first time I had looked at both her eyes. Somehow that was more important to me than anything—being able to look into her eyes.

The one that had gone blind didn't look any different. All the damage, she said, was way at the back, where it didn't show.

"Wouldn't it be nice," she said, "if I could just go to the camera store and get a new film?" But that was all she said about it.

We didn't talk much about Ruthie. I wasn't up to that, and she knew it without my saying so. Instead she told me a story I had never heard before. I wondered if even Mom knew it, but I never asked her.

She said that about five years before Mom was born, she had had another baby by her first husband. A little girl. She lived to be a little over three. She died of spinal meningitis, very quickly.

Nonny was telling me this in a quiet, almost matter-of-fact voice, no drama. "She was a beautiful child. Dark curly hair and big dark eyes with gold specks. A beautiful child." She looked down at the menu. I could tell she was trying not to sound emotional. She just wanted me to know about this.

The waitress appeared. Nonny turned on her famous charm, and we ordered our lunch. I could tell the waitress recognized her.

I wasn't sure if I should say anything. But I did. I said, "What was her name?"

She gave me a little smile I'll never forget. "Mary Lee."

I almost burst into tears. I had been named for Nonny's dead child. Either Mom knew about her or Nonny had asked her to name me Lee.

"My marriage to George broke up after that. It was quite irrational—the poor man had nothing to do with Mary Lee's death—but after that I couldn't bear to look at him."

"How can I live up to that?" I said. It frightened me. That perfect child, and I was her namesake.

"No, no." She put her hand over mine. "It's not like that. You are another person. You just live up to being Lee McDougall. That's enough for me."

Our lunch came, and I guess it was very good—Nonny said it was—but I can't remember anything we ate.

During dessert she said, "I hope I'm doing the right thing for Savannah. I have a bad habit of arranging other people's lives." She laughed a dry little laugh. "As your mother can tell you."

"I've thought about Savannah a lot," I said. "I think it's right for her. I know she has real talent, because she almost made me cry in that play. And I'm not into being sentimental about my sister." I played with the spoon. "Although things have changed. She saved four of my wolves, and I know how terrified she was to go in there."

"Savannah has strength," Nonny said. "Both of you have. I count on that."

Eric had gone off to have his lunch somewhere, but he was waiting when we came out. He and Nonny had agreed that he would drive the limo all the way in to the cabin, and they'd been doing that for a couple of days. "If it gets scratched," Nonny told him, "I'll pay for a paint job. I'm not up to walking that last half mile, like Gretel into the dark woods."

Nonny did some last-minute errands, and then both she and Eric stayed at our house for dinner. Mom had knocked herself out roasting duck, stuffing baked potatoes, and making a fabulous salad. Everybody tried hard to be cheerful. It helped having Eric there; nobody was going to get too personal or emotional, although my dad was having trouble staying calm. He was torn between the excitement and pride in having his beloved Vannie move into the circles of the great, and losing her.

I tried not to think of Ruthie, and I almost made it, until Nonny went out alone to say good-bye to the wolves. I had to go into my room for a few minutes.

CHAPTER 37

Their flight was a minute before midnight, so we had the day to get through. Nonny was to meet us at the turnoff to the main road at 9:15 P.M. Van and I would go in the limo.

When I went out to feed the wolves and play with them for a while, I went over and filled in Ruthie's den. I didn't want anybody else using it. The other wolves had made a den of their own, on the other side of the woods. I avoided going near it, because I wasn't sure they wanted me to.

Later, coming up the path to the house, I heard Savannah and Mom talking. Savannah's voice carries ("projection, projection!"), but Mom's is quiet, unless she's angry or wants to make a point. In a different way her voice is as beautiful as Nonny's.

"I'd like to have your blue Chinese ginger jar," Savannah was saying.

"What for?"

"Well, I had this neat idea. If you'll run me over to the vet's, I'll get Ruthie's ashes and put them in the jar, and Lee and I can hold a burial ceremony. Maybe at Ruthie's old den . . ."

I stormed up the path into the house. "No way!" I yelled at her. "Don't you dare touch Ruthie's ashes. Anyway, they're gone."

"Well, we could put some dirt in the jar and pretend. We could say a prayer and—"

"Ruthie is not a handful of dirt in the ground, or ashes either!" I was yelling.

"Hey, calm down, Lee," Savannah said. "I thought since you loved her so much, you'd want something to remember her by."

"I've *got* something to remember her by. Inside of me. You mind your own business." For the first time since Ruthie died, I burst into tears and ran into my room.

I heard Savannah say, "I was just trying to be nice."

And my mother saying, "Vannie, you have to learn that trying to be nice is not always the kindest thing to do."

There was a long pause. Then Savannah said, "Oh."

We avoided each other for a couple of hours, me by staying out in the woods while she finished last-minute packing. Then she came out.

"I left some winter sweaters," she said. "If you want them. If not, Mom will take them to Goodwill."

"I'd like that Norwegian one."

"It's there. Help yourself." She had come into the wolf enclosure, not acting nervous at all. Silver pushed up against her, wanting her head scratched. She seldom did that to me.

"She likes you," I said.

Savannah stroked the wolf's head, and shooed Snow away from her shoes. "They're nice, aren't they?"

"Yes, they are."

"Why are people scared of them?"

"Nonny says it's some ancient myth, nobody knows where it came from. There might have been a strain of primitive animals millions of years ago that were fierce, and maybe wolves descended from them or looked like them."

"Like Neanderthal man and us." She leaned over, smoothing the thick silvery fur on Silver's back. "Hey, I'm sorry about—"

I interrupted her. "No problem. I guess I was ready to blow my cool."

"I only thought—"

"I know you did. Thanks for the thought. Are you and I going to ride in the limo, for sure?"

"I think so. Dad wanted me to ride with them, but I wanted to go with you and Nonny. And Eric. He's kind of neat, isn't he?"

"Kind of old for you."

"I'm not going to be twelve forever."

"That's a fact." Eighteen, any minute now, I thought.

We rode into town with Mom and had lunch, and got the things Savannah had forgotten, like toothpaste and a whole box of Heath bars—as if they wouldn't have them in Laguna.

"Nonny's got four people already enrolled in her acting class," Savannah said. "I make five. She'll close it at eight."

"It will probably be more hard work than glamour," Mom said, "if memory serves me."

Savannah lifted her chin. "Hard work is the ladder to success."

Mom and I exchanged grins. Guess where she got that quote.

"An actress," Savannah went on, "has to suffer before she can be any good."

In the bookstore she collected some magazines to read on the plane: *People, Seventeen, Glamour.* She was disappointed because he didn't have *Weekly Variety.*

Suddenly my sister seemed awfully young, and I was scared she'd be grown up by Christmas and not the same person at all. I bought her a copy of *Cricket.*

She looked at me as if I were crazy, or making fun of her.

"Lest we forget," I said, and she laughed, although she still looked baffled.

Time began to speed up after we got back to the cabin. There were so many last-minute things to do. We ate a fast, simple supper, nobody talking much.

And then it was time to drive out to the highway and meet the limo. I rode in back with Nonny, and Savannah was up front, asking Eric a million questions about law school and his girlfriends and life in Chicago, where he came from.

Nonny held my hand, and we didn't talk much. It was raining, and the ride took a little longer than usual. Savannah worried about fog closing in the airport.

"That's only in winter," I told her.

When we drove into Johnson-Bell Airport, we found Dad and Mom, Dad looking pleased with himself because he'd beat the limo by ten minutes.

We stood around while Eric brought in the luggage, checked it, and gave Nonny the tickets; then he carried her little overnight case as we all went over to gate four. I think he was really sorry to say good-bye to her. Nonny is great to work for as long as you do what she says. Only her secretary, who's been with her for years, can talk back to her.

She gave Eric a check for the car rental and told him to get in touch if the owner wanted her to pay for repainting. It did have a few scratches and one deepish gouge. Then she tucked a folded bill in his jacket pocket. It looked to me like a hundred.

"That's between you and me," she said, "for a job well done."

He blushed and thanked her and shook hands with all of us and left.

"Nice lad," she said. And probably never thought of him again.

The plane was on time, already waiting. There were only five other passengers. Nonny and Savannah hugged each of us, and we all tried to act casual, like "see you in a couple of days."

They were next in line to show their tickets at the gate when Savannah broke away, ran to me, and hugged me again. In my ear she said, "I love you. Don't change." And she was gone before I could answer. I had a big lump in my throat.

Mom and Dad waited in the upstairs section, where

they could see the little plane take off, but I went outside and walked up and down in the rain.

I heard the engine revving up, and rain-streaked light covered the field as the plane taxied to the end of the short runway, where the mountains seem to loom right in front of your face.

Then there was that heart-stopping roar when the plane has paused and is about to take off. I shut my eyes and crossed my fingers. Takeoffs scare me.

It was up, climbing fast and circling the field, graceful as a small hawk. It didn't make that heavy drone the big planes make, but you could hear it over the splatter of rain. I shielded my face with my hand. It had completed the circle and straightened out, heading west, blinking away like a firefly that didn't know enough to come in out of the rain.

Nonny says it's bad luck to wish an actor good luck; they say "Break a leg." So break a leg, my sister.

When Dad unlocked the car, I curled up in the back-seat. Just before I fell asleep, I thought that, the way Thunder and Prometheus had been playing up to Silver lately, we'd probably have two or three baby wolves in the spring, maybe more. But you were the first, Ruthie. Lupe, Queen of the Forest.

CHAPTER 38

Savannah had been gone four days. Mom and I were sitting on the front steps, shucking corn and telling each other how much more we missed her than we had thought we would.

"The cabin seems darker somehow," I said.

Mom smiled. "That might have something to do with the fact that it's fall."

"School day after tomorrow."

"One more new school for you. Do you mind?"

"Not really. If we had always lived in Missoula, I'd still have had changes: elementary, middle school, high school."

Mom looked up. She is quicker at hearing things than I am. Somebody on a bike had ridden up to our new fence. I shaded my eyes to see better.

"Oh, no," I said. "It's that nutty stage manager. The one Savannah said was rich. Can you believe it?"

He was wearing his Serengeti shades and his baseball cap, white shorts, and a bright green tank top.

"Hello!" he hollered. "Can I come in?"

"Come ahead," Mom called back.

He left his bike on one side of the trail, opened the gate, and loped in on those long, skinny legs.

"Hi, Lee," he said, like we were old buddies. "Mrs. McDougall, I'm Doug Waterson. I was stage manager at the theater."

"Savannah has spoken of you."

"I think it's great that she has a chance to study with her grandmother. I've seen some of Savannah Saxton's films. She's terrific." He sat down on the lower step and said, "I heard about Ruthie, and I don't know how to tell you how bad I feel."

I was touched. He looked as if he meant it, and he had called Ruthie by name. Maybe he wasn't such a jerk as I'd thought.

"Do you like wolves?" Mom said.

"Mrs. McDougall, I love wolves. When I was a kid growing up in Denver, I went to a zoo and saw this big Arctic wolf pacing up and down in a cage. Just a lousy small cage. He was so beautiful, so much dignity. . . . It nearly killed me to see him in that humiliating position. I went every week for a long time, and I wrote tons of letters to the paper and to the zoo to get him out of that cage. One day he was gone, and I could never find out where he went"—he shook his head—"today, believe me, I'd find out. But I've been hooked on wolves ever since."

I'd been wrong about this guy. "Would you like to see my wolves?"

"Oh, I'd love to. I've been wanting all summer to get over here. If you'd let me, I mean. But I never could get away."

I took him into the wolf area. As usual, they had faded away. We sat down on the big log where I do my sketching and waited.

He wanted to know about the guys poisoning the wolves. There had been a brief story in the paper, but the police had asked us to keep it low-key. They were still looking for Sawyer and the others. I told him the story, and that it was hush-hush for now.

"I understand." He tensed and said in a low voice, "Oh, look!"

Thunder had silently come out of the trees into the open, looking us over, keeping his distance.

"Oh, my gosh," Doug said, almost under his breath.

I don't think I'd ever heard anybody say "my gosh" except on "Leave It to Beaver" reruns. I kind of liked it. He seemed old-fashioned in a funny, nice way. Wow, had I ever been wrong.

Neither of us said anything while the other three came out of the woods. Of course Prometheus trotted right up close, gave him a few quick sniffs, and began to untie the mismatched laces on his old running shoes. Doug was completely charmed. He could hardly speak. He sat as if he were under some magic spell while Silver and Snow sniffed the back of his neck and tugged at his shirt.

Mom came out with three Cokes. He took one and

thanked her, but I don't think he even knew what he was doing.

"You have to watch them," Mom said as Silver pulled on his shorts. "They'll take all your clothes off if you let them. They think it's a big joke."

Just as she said that, Snow caught the bow of Doug's glasses in his teeth and pulled them off.

"Whoa!" Doug was laughing. "Those are prescription, man. I'm blind as a bat without 'em."

I rescued them for him. He had blue eyes.

"Thanks," he said. "Nearsighted. Listen, Lee, you plan to keep these wolves, right?"

"Of course."

"I figured you did; otherwise you wouldn't have taken so many risks with the antiwolf monsters. What about pups? Silver's bound to have some."

"The more, the merrier," I said.

"What about when you go to school, and later when you go to college? What are your plans?"

"My mother is as involved with them as I am." I told him about her biology project. He knew the professor she was working with.

"He's a great guy. I'm majoring in wildlife management, but I've had a lot of biology, of course. He was my prof for the advanced courses."

He and Mom talked about the professor and what she planned to do.

Mom invited him to dinner. It wasn't easy getting him into the house, away from the wolves, but once he was inside he suddenly got very businesslike.

"I got so excited about the wolves, I'm forgetting what I came for. But first let me be quite sure we're seeing this the same way. You're serious about the wolves, right? Over the long haul?"

I didn't answer for a minute because I was trying to think how to say it. "I think I've known since I got them that this was what I've been looking for. But the night my sister forgot to be scared and saved them for me, I knew that she knew they meant to me what acting means to her." I looked at Mom, and she smiled. "I want to go to the university and take some biology, but mostly English, because what I want to do is write books about wolves so kids will see they aren't scary."

"Good. Mrs. McDougall, you listen to this too, because you're part of it."

Mom sat down at the table with us.

"My grandfather left me a lot of money. It's gross to talk about your money but I have to, to explain this. First I was going to use it to start a theater of my own. Theater is my second passion. But then a couple of my friends and I got together and formed a group—we call it Wolves Unlimited—and we work in cooperation with Defenders of Wildlife. Only what we do is buy up suitable property that's going cheap, like the Sawyer place, where people can raise wolves."

I was stunned. "You don't mean *you* bought that place?"

"My group, yeah. And our idea was that you could use that land as your pack grows. There are no strings attached, even though I've asked you so many questions. If you ever decide you don't want the land—or the wolves—we'll find another wolf family."

Mom was as surprised as I was about the land, and relieved.

"Wouldn't Arthur Washington be pleased," she said.

He stared at her. "Wait a minute! Are you going to tell me these are Washington's wolves?"

I told him about it.

"Well, I'll be doggoned! At least half a dozen times I tried to see those wolves, but Washington wouldn't let anybody near them." He couldn't get over his amazement. "I was going to ask you where you did get them. You know, when I saw Savannah on the tube talking about Ruthie, I got our director to give her a walk-on, so I could find out more. But she never wanted to talk about them."

This time Mom and I were astonished. "You mean," I said, "Ruthie got Savannah her job?"

"I guess you could say that."

Mom and I looked at each other. "Don't ever tell her," Mom said.

"Of course she was a very pretty girl and as it turned out, she had talent. But that was a lucky break for all of us."

Dad got home about then, and we had to go through all the introductions and explanations, except the part about Ruthie getting Savannah her job. Dad was fascinated. I think he's always kind of fascinated by millionaires, which was what Doug apparently was.

"The other thing is," Doug said while we were having dinner, "I'm doing kind of a preliminary report for Defenders of Wildlife. Their guy will be out to see you. I don't know if you know this, but they will give five thousand dollars to anyone who has space enough and cares enough to take on some wolves, a pair or even a single female if she's pregnant, and agrees to raise the pups and take care of them."

My father was almost falling off his chair. "Did you say five thousand dollars? Did I hear you say that?"

Doug laughed. "Yes, sir, you heard me right. They've advertised it, but I guess a lot of people haven't heard about it."

Dad looked at me. "Lee," he said, "guard those wolves with your life."

"Dad," I said. "Where've you been? That's what I've been planning to do all along."

Dad gave me his biggest grin. "That's my girl," he said.

READING LIST

Brandenberg, Jim. *White Wolf.* Minoqua, Wis.: Northwood Press, 1988.

Johnson, Sylvia A., and Alice Aamodt. *Wolf Pack: Tracking Wolves in the Wild.* Minneapolis: Lerner Publications, 1985.

Lawrence, R. D. *In Praise of Wolves.* New York: Ballantine Books, 1986.

————. *Secret Go the Wolves.* New York: Ballantine Books, 1980.

Mech, L. David. *The Wolf.* Garden City, N.Y.: Natural History Press, 1970.

————. *The Arctic Wolf.* Stillwater, Minn.: Voyageur Press, 1988.

Wolves in American Culture Committee. *Wolf!* Boise, Idaho: Boise State University Press, 1986.